LARKSPUR HOUSE

Dear Friend,

You ~~HAVE TO COME HELP US~~ are cordially invited to a house ~~THAT WANTS TO SCARE YOU~~ unlike any you've ever entered——one that understands your wishes and dreams, and wants to ~~KEEP YOU FOREVER~~ help make them come true.

Few have been called ~~AND EVEN FEWER ESCAPE,~~ but if you're reading this, you're one of the Special ones. Come. Let's play.

Most sincerely,

~~Larkspur~~ *SHADOW HOUSE*

Enter Shadow House . . . if you dare.

1. Get the FREE Shadow House app for your phone or tablet.
2. Each image in the book reveals a ghost story in the app.
3. Step into ghost stories, where the choices you make determine your fate.

 For tablet or phone.

scholastic.com/shadowhouse

SHADOW HOUSE

The Missing

SHADOW HOUSE

The Missing

DAN POBLOCKI

SCHOLASTIC INC.

For my mentor and friend, David Levithan.

CHAPTER 1

VOICES ECHOED UP from below.

It was long past midnight, but Jason's parents were fighting again.

"I cannot believe you think I'd do something like that," said his mom.

His dad spat back, "It's like you care more about *that old toy* than you do your own daughter."

His mom and dad grew louder, angrier, and Jason cringed, pulling the thin blanket up to his chin.

"Why would I lie? I want to protect Louise as much as you do!"

"If you'd actually brought the dollhouse to the children's home yesterday, why did Louise find it back in her bedroom this afternoon?"

"I have no clue! The director at the home was thrilled to have it. You can call her yourself!"

"It's the middle of the night, Amy! Everyone is asleep!"

Well, not *everyone* . . .

Jason covered his ears, trying to block out the noise. His mom and dad must have known how loud they were being. It was like they wanted him to hear everything—as if the argument would force him to pick a side. Lou too. He pictured his little sister just down the hallway, huddled in her own bed, guilt wracking her small frame. Ever since she'd started sleepwalking, their usually peaceful home had grown toxic, as if a hidden, leaking pipe were rotting the walls. Jason riffled through one of the many catalogs he kept stored in his mind, thinking of the different kinds of mold he'd studied in his science class.

1. *Penicillium*
2. *Trichoderma*
3. *Aspergillus*

"I'm as freaked out about it as you are, Scott." Mom's voice cracked. "How do I know that *you* didn't go to the city and bring the dollhouse back here?"

Jason crept out of bed and pressed his ear against the door.

He sensed someone standing on the other side.

He swung the door open quickly to find his sister in the darkness. Her long black hair partially obscured her pale face as she clutched at her torso. "Lou! Are you sleepwalking again?" he whispered.

The argument continued from the kitchen below.

"Not anymore," said Lou. "Can I stay with you for a little while? At least until they calm down?"

Together, they perched on the edge of his bed. Lou squeezed Jason's hand, and her chilled fingers sent goose bumps up his arm. "Are you okay? You've never actually sleepwalked *out* of the house before. Good thing Dad was up late watching television, or else you might have ended up—"

"I don't want to think about that," Lou said, taking back her hand.

"Was it the kids in the dollhouse?" Jason whispered.

"Same as always. But this time, in my dream, I was with them. And the creature . . . it was chasing *all* of us."

"It was just a nightmare, Lou. Those kids aren't real."

"Maybe not. But the dollhouse sure is." She released a ragged sigh. "Mom and Dad are right to be scared. How did it come back? I went with Mom to donate it!"

"One of them must have—"

"You know that's not true, Jay." Lou shook her head. "Something else is going on here—something . . . not right."

"At least the dollhouse is in the basement now. Dad made sure of that after he brought you back inside from your sleepy hike."

This made Lou smile. "Yeah, I heard him thumping it all the way down the stairs."

"Maybe it broke."

The dollhouse had once belonged to their mother. It stood almost three feet high and was nearly as wide as the antique trunk in the hall closet, where Mom kept extra bed linens. The roofline was filled with sharp points made of gables, turrets, and spires. The outside of the house was painted gray and black, and was covered in tall, skinny windows that made Jason think of ancient, haunted fortresses. And whenever anyone unlatched the dollhouse and swung it open, the hinges would squeal like a terrified animal pinned down by a hungry predator. Its rooms were linked in a confusing jumble— the total opposite of the simple, streamlined condo where the Benjamins lived. The dollhouse had always given Jason the heebie-jeebies, but now that it was haunting his sister's dreams, he wished that his mom had never inherited it.

Lou backed away. He heard a quiver in her voice as she said, "I'd be happy if I never had to look at it again."

A phone call pulled Jason out of a dreamless sleep, and when he wandered to the kitchen, he found his parents pacing. The anger of the previous night had been replaced by worry.

"What now?" asked Jason, thinking of the dollhouse. "Is Lou okay?"

"She's still in bed," said Dad.

His mom took his hands and sat him down. "Aunt Paige just called from Ohio. Your cousin Marcus is missing."

Jason felt something in his chest tighten. "But we just saw him a few months ago." Dad covered his face with his hands. Jason realized how silly he must sound. Every day, people see each other for the last time.

Mom continued. "Aunt Paige said that yesterday morning, he was simply . . . gone. He'd taken his cello and a bag with some clothes. They think he might have run away."

"But why?"

"I don't know, honey. But your aunt needs my support. I'm booking a flight to Ohio this afternoon. And I'm taking Lou with me."

Jason flinched. "Lou?"

Dad chimed in. "It might be good for your sister to get away from Walnut Creek for a while."

Jason sensed that there were other reasons hidden inside his father's first reason: *It might be good for your sister to get away from the dollhouse in the basement.* Also: *It might be good for all of us to have some time apart.*

CHAPTER 2

LOU WAS AFRAID to fall asleep on the plane, but the engines whirred in her ears and she caught herself nodding off several times. In the few moments of creeping unconsciousness, she could hear screaming and creaking doors and footsteps coming up quickly behind her . . . echoes of the familiar nightmare that had woken her so many nights over the last month.

Then the plane was braking hard, throwing her body forward, the lap belt catching her before she could smash into the seat in front of her. Outside, past all the roads and fields, a dense line of foliage revealed land that was almost totally flat. Quite a difference from the rolling hills and mountains around the Bay Area.

Mom leaned over and whispered in her ear, "We made it, honey. Safe and sound."

The words *safe and sound* made Lou think of her cousin, and for a second, she felt nauseated, knowing that Marcus might be neither of those things.

When they got to the Gellers' house, Aunt Paige pulled Lou's mom into a long hug. "We're so glad you're here!" she said, her voice cracking a little. "The police have been in the house all morning, and we don't know what to do. What could have happened?"

Marcus's oldest brother chimed in. "The little freak is probably just hiding out somewhere, practicing his cello."

Aunt Paige's expression hardened, and she turned to Lou. "Thank you for coming," she said. "It means a whole lot. Ethan, show your cousin up to Marcus's room."

Late daylight streamed through gauzy curtains upstairs. Lou plopped her suitcase on the floor and stared around. It felt strange to be in here when Marcus was not. A blue button-down shirt hung on the back of his desk chair, and colored pencils were scattered across the surface of the desk. Several keys on the electric piano in the corner of the room appeared to be smudged with remnants of purple Popsicle melt. A stack of books sat crookedly on the bedside table—*The House with a Clock in Its Walls* by John Bellairs, *Coraline* by Neil Gaiman, *50 Simple Magic Tricks to Entertain Your Friends and Family*, and a dog-eared biography of a jazz musician named Dave Brubeck.

Lou sat on the bed and cracked the book about magic tricks. One page in the center stuck as she flipped through it. Someone had placed a piece of folded paper inside, and Lou opened it. The email was addressed to Aunt Paige.

Dear Mrs. Geller,

My name is L. Delphinium, and I am the director of the Larkspur Academy for the Performing Arts in New York State. I work with several professional scouts around the world and when one of them attended your son's recent recital at the Oberlin campus in Ohio, she was overcome by the power of his performance. We would love it if Marcus came to study with us . . .

Lou read the email over and over, trying to make sense of it. Could this be the answer to where Marcus was? Did Aunt Paige not remember receiving the email? Maybe Marcus had gotten it directly and had never showed it to her. But Marcus didn't seem like the type to just take off for a music camp in New York without his parents being on board.

Downstairs, horror dawned on Aunt Paige's face as she scanned the page. "Where did you get this?"

Lou worried that she'd made a mistake. "It was stuck in a book by Marcus's bed."

Aunt Paige showed the printout to Lou's mother, who gasped, "Call the detective!"

"This has got to be some sort of joke," Aunt Paige went on, as if talking to herself. "Larkspur Academy?"

"*Larkspur.* You don't think . . ." Mom trailed off before glancing at Lou and then pulling her sister away into the kitchen. The two women whispered, and Lou crept to the doorway to catch what they were saying.

She could only hear snippets. "That old mansion burned down years ago, long before Mom and Dad left Greencliffe. Even before Shane went missing . . ."

Lou knew that Shane had been Mom and Aunt Paige's brother, and that he'd died when he was young, but no one ever talked about him. At least not around her. Lou leaned closer.

"Maybe the Caldwell family rebuilt it."

"I don't think any of them survived the fire."

"Still, it doesn't answer why Marcus would have hidden the email from me . . ."

Her mother gasped, and Lou jolted, covering her mouth to keep from squeaking. "You don't think this has anything to do with our old dollhouse, do you?"

"The dollhouse?"

"Yes! Gramma was always so proud that it came from Larkspur House . . ."

Lou clutched at the door frame, her head spinning. The dollhouse had come from a place called Larkspur? Her mother caught a glimpse of her. "Louise . . . honey, why don't you go sit with your cousins."

Aunt Paige was making a call. "Yes, Detective Dosteler? This is Paige Geller . . . thank you. Listen, my niece found some information that I think you need to see . . . Now? Yes, I can bring it to the station right away."

Lou sat in front of the television as the sun sank past the horizon. She couldn't fathom Marcus spending another night without his family, and it felt like they'd made no progress in finding him.

Eventually, she crept upstairs and turned on the family's computer in the alcove over the front door. Logging on to her messenger account, she found that Jason was also online.

11

She mentioned what was going on with the email printout, and Mom and Aunt Paige's conversation about *Larkspur*.

You found a clue! he wrote back. *Nice work, Detective!*

How's everything in Walnut Creek? Miss me?

You wish, he teased. *It's finally quiet around here.*

She knew he was joking, but still, it stung.

Tired from the flight and the lack of sleep the previous night, she stretched out on Marcus's comforter and closed her eyes. Her stomach grumbled. Uncle Gilbert had said he'd order pizza. She hoped that he hadn't forgotten. She thought about flipping through the book about magic tricks, but she couldn't stop thinking about five children running through the dollhouse and the shifting mass of shadow that chased them. Before she knew it, the words on the page blurred and shadows swirled as her eyelids grew heavy and her head began to nod.

In California, Jason enjoyed an evening of peace and quiet in his bedroom. His sister's dollhouse was locked in the basement storage room two floors below, and it felt as though the bizarre energy that lived inside the condo was gone now.

According to Lou, Marcus had secretly made his way to a music academy in New York. Jason knew that his cousin loved music and was kind of a cello prodigy, but he had never taken Marcus to be adventurous. To travel alone across the country without even telling your parents? That was actually kinda *punk*.

If it were true, the police would probably find Marcus within the next couple of hours. Mom and Lou would have a nice visit and then come home. And Jason could focus on his summer science project, mapping the ecosystems surrounding Mount Diablo. It made him feel good to keep organized, to know where everything fit. It helped him understand how he fit in too. He opened a folder on his computer containing photographs he'd taken of plants and animals while hiking in the parks, and then began to organize the images into categories.

1. *Elevation*
2. *Habitat type*
3. *Predators*
4. *Prey*

After a moment, he thought of a new category.

5. *Environmental dangers*

Brush fires. Earthquakes. Drought. Floods . . . *Dollhouses and nightmares.*

Lately, it seemed that anything could happen, and nowhere was safe.

There was a knock at the bedroom door. Jason turned to find his father standing in the hall. His face looked gray. Something was very, very wrong. When Jason stood, his chair tumbled over backward and whacked against the floor.

The noise snapped Dad out of his spell. He rushed into the room and threw his arms around Jason, squeezing so hard that Jason couldn't catch his breath. He managed to ask, "What happened?"

"Lou is gone. Missing. Just like Marcus."

Jason felt like someone had removed his skin, the cool air in his bedroom biting directly into his flesh. "That's not . . . I just chatted . . . You're joking!"

"I wouldn't joke about this," Dad said. "Your mother went upstairs to get Lou for dinner and found Marcus's room empty. The Gellers searched the whole house and the yard and the neighborhood. The police came, but they found nothing."

"Do they think someone took her?" Jason choked out.

Dad shook his head violently. "They don't know. The first available flight to Ohio isn't until early tomorrow morning. I booked tickets for us. Pack a bag so we can just get up and go."

Later, in bed, darkness throbbed at the corners of Jason's vision. His lungs felt like they'd shriveled. In his mind, he tried to list places where Lou could be hiding, but he didn't know Marcus's neighborhood well enough. If she were here, he'd scream at her for frightening all of them, mentioning all the reasons she should never do it again.

1. *I'm scared*
2. *I'm scared*
3. *I'm scared*
4. *I'm—*

Something crawled across his cheek. Jason bolted upright, imagining spiders. When he wiped at his face, his fingers came away wet. The tears only made him angrier.

"*Jason . . .*"

It was a whisper from the hallway. Jason opened the door and peered around the corner. The voice called, louder, as if from the mudroom near the condo's back staircase. *"Jason . . ."*

"Dad?" Jason called out. "Did you hear that?"

But his father didn't answer. Jason made his way down the hall. His father's door was locked, and when Jason knocked, his father didn't answer.

"Shhh . . ." The voice came again. This was followed by the squeaking of the mudroom's door.

"Louise? Is that you?" But he knew it wasn't.

Footsteps pattered down the stairs, and Jason ran to keep up. Glancing out into the lighted stairwell, Jason saw a shadow disappear around the lowest landing.

"Hurry!"

This time the voice was clear and present and totally real. It echoed up the chamber, pulling Jason forward. Barefoot, he raced down the steps as if the owner of the voice might get away along with all the answers he'd need to ever get to sleep again.

Down and down and down he went. Past the first floor, toward the basement.

It wasn't until he was standing in front of its open door that he realized the voice had called him to the storage room. His father had warned him and Lou that neither was to open it.

Darkness flickered inside.

After a few seconds, Jason's eyes began to adjust. Against the far wall, perched in shadow like a hidden beast, was the dollhouse.

"*Come in,*" the voice whispered.

CHAPTER 3

JASON SWIPED AT the wall inside the door, but he couldn't find the switch. A sliver of light beamed from the stairwell.

"Hello?" Jason tried to take a deep breath, but his chest refused to expand. Tightness at his temples made him squint. He crept past shadowed cardboard boxes that were stuffed with Hanukkah decorations and baby clothes and old books and art projects from when he was little. The boxes were stacked neatly in several rows.

The dollhouse was straight ahead. In the dark, it seemed larger than it did in Lou's bedroom. The roofline was pointier, with several more towers and turrets than he remembered. Was it a trick of the light?

Between his own shallow breaths, he could hear someone else breathing too. He closed off his throat, trying to
pinpoint where it was coming from. It sounded as though
someone was on the other side of the dollhouse, but that was
impossible. Just behind it, a cinder block wall rose up from
the basement's concrete floor.

Jason was about to turn around when every window of
the dollhouse at his feet blinked to life and a cool glow
spilled out.

He stumbled backward and then scrambled toward the
storage room's door, but the boxes were gone now, and so was
the light from the stairwell. He couldn't tell where he was.

Jason shouted for his father, but only silence answered
him. As the darkness expanded in all directions, he spoke to
himself instead. "Wake up, Jason . . . Please . . ."

Something brushed against his cheek. This time, it wasn't
tears. He spun, waving his hands blindly. A wet slap hit the
floor behind him, and his chest constricted. He leapt away,
realizing for the first time that he was barefoot. The floor was
no longer smooth concrete, but gritty and pockmarked and
damp, like he was outside. Something dragged itself toward
him, slithering quickly over his toes, leaving behind a
warm stickiness. He clamped his throat shut to keep from

shrieking. He pictured the photos of insects and snakes and furry things with claws and fangs that he'd been organizing for his science project.

This had to be a dream. A very bad dream. And all he had to do was wake up . . .

"Jason!" The voice was calling from somewhere far behind him. It was no longer a whisper. Now it belonged to a young girl—high and sweet, like a song. "This way!"

He scanned the darkness and found a pinpoint glow in the distance. It was a singular and unmoving spark, like someone had punched a hole in a giant piece of black construction paper and was shining a powerful spotlight from behind it. That was where the voice was coming from— hundreds of feet away. "Hurry!" Jason raced toward it, his bare feet pounding against the uneven ground. Sounds of scrabbling and scraping followed him. The pinpoint glow grew brighter. Hope swelled in his chest until he realized what he was running toward.

The dollhouse.

How had the distance grown so far? Unless this was like Lou's nightmare . . . Unless . . .

He didn't want to come any closer to it, but he sensed the things in the dark creeping toward him. He imagined:

1. *Claws*
2. *Rank breath*
3. *Teeth made for breaking bones and tearing into muscle*

His mouth agape, Jason ran faster than he'd ever done during gym class. If Mr. Lingnofski were timing him, he knew he'd have broken some sort of record. He approached the glow that beamed from inside the dollhouse's windows, and then he skidded to a halt. His sister's toy was only a few feet away now. There was nowhere else to go, nowhere to run.

To his relief, the sounds that had followed him faded away—grunts and scraping footfalls retreated into the dark. He swung out at the shadows. "Stay away from me!" he called out, before bending over, heaving breath, trying to not vomit.

A few moments later, he straightened his spine and listened for the voice that had saved him, as if it might be whispering to him from nearby.

Instead, Jason heard other voices. Frightened voices. They came from inside the house. Crouching, he peered through the slim windows. There appeared to be several dolls scattered throughout the maze of rooms and halls inside. One of the dolls caught his eye. It had pale skin and long, dark hair. It looked exactly like his sister.

The sight of it knocked away his breath again. "Louise . . . ," he whispered. His voice echoed around him, and he felt foolish. Then the figure moved. Jason nearly toppled over. The doll that looked like his sister actually walked through a parlor, shuffling her feet in his sister's familiar gait.

Was this really happening? Could he trust his own eyes? Even if this was a bad dream, there had to be some logic to it. Right? *Talk to her. Ask her what's going on . . .*

"L-Lou? Can you hear me?"

She paid no attention but continued to look around the space, dragging her tiny fingertips across miniature marble busts, as if collecting dust.

"Lou!" he yelled. Again, no response.

"Hello?" Another voice came from another part of the house. It was another tiny girl whose skin was brown, with hair even darker than Lou's. It was brushed high in the front and pinned up on the sides before falling in long curls to her shoulders. Her short-sleeved, red-and-white polka-dot dress revealed long, thin arms. She stood stiffly in the center of a large bathroom. An elegant claw-foot bathtub sat on top of black-and-white tiles, which were laid out in intricate diamonds across the floor. "Is this a joke?" asked the girl. "I don't find it funny! Mama! Auntie Kerani! Where did you go?"

Several rooms away, a boy who was much bigger than either of the girls crept around on his tiptoes. He wore baggy black shorts and a short-sleeved black button-down cowboy shirt. His cropped hair was spiked up in the front. His eyes were dark and wide, but he didn't say a word. In fact, as he moved throughout what looked like a child's nursery, the boy didn't make a sound.

On the level where Lou continued to wander, another girl was walking through a room with indigo wallpaper. Her brown hair was divided in the middle and fell to her shoulders in two braids.

In an adjacent room, a blond boy disappeared through a doorway before Jason made out what he looked like.

His conversation with Lou from the previous night echoed in his head: *The kids in the dollhouse . . .*

Had his sister become one of them?

CHAPTER 4

LOU STARTLED AWAKE to find herself on a blue velvet daybed in an ornately decorated room that seemed vaguely familiar. White marble busts stood atop tall pedestals around the space—a young woman whose face was covered by a transparent veil, an older gentleman whose ruffled shirt collar made him look important and ridiculous, a grand dame whose hair was coiled in braids atop her head, and more. In the corner stood a white stone statue of a girl dressed in a simple robe holding out a book. The empty eyes seemed to stare.

Lou blinked and wiped at her own eyes, certain that she was dreaming. The longer she remained asleep, the more time her brain would have to throw something terrifying into the mix.

Usually, whenever Lou wondered if she was inside a nightmare, she'd pinch the skin between her thumb and forefinger, and almost immediately she'd find herself lying in bed, the dull pain throbbing toward her wrist.

Lou sat up and tried it now. It hurt, but as seconds ticked by, she realized she was still perched on the same daybed in the same room.

Lou knew then that she wasn't asleep. Her heart fluttered and her tongue went dry. Frustrated, she stood and wandered between the busts.

When she'd made it halfway across the room, she noticed a golden frame hanging on the wall between two windows. The picture inside the frame was one she'd drawn for the dollhouse a couple of years prior, of a vase full of lilies. When Lou had finished it, the drawing had been minuscule. This one, however, was several feet high.

"Am I . . . am I *inside* the dollhouse?" A spot on her forehead went cold with fear before spreading chills across her scalp.

There was a scraping sound beside her. Lou turned to find the bust of the veiled woman facing her. Suddenly, the veiled woman smiled, showing wet, ruby-colored teeth. Lou screamed and pushed at the pedestal. The stone seemed to push back at her.

Something pounded at the window. A giant fingertip was at the glass, *tap-tap-tapping*. At any moment, it might smash through and come jousting at her. Lou's legs nearly gave out. An enormous eye appeared in the frame. As she peered back, the eye pulled away and revealed a gigantic face that looked like Jason's. He opened his mouth. Strands of spittle stretched from the top teeth to the bottom. Lou sprinted toward a door on the far wall and discovered a small closet space. Hopping inside, she closed the door again and shivered as she held it tight.

Was she dead? Had the plane crashed before reaching Cleveland? Maybe this was what it felt like to be a ghost: left behind by the whole world, forgotten inside a nightmare. Her lungs hitched as she squeezed the doorknob harder.

The walls of the cramped space began to vibrate. A sound emerged from inside the vibration. A growl.

Lou couldn't stop herself from screaming.

CHAPTER 5

JASON HAD ONLY wanted to get his sister's attention, but when he saw the look of horror on her tiny face, he realized his mistake. "Lou!" he called. But she'd closed herself into a closet. "It's only me . . . Come out!"

To her, he must have looked like some kind of monster.

Something inside the dollhouse was making a horrible noise—a rumbling growl. If Lou hadn't been frightened before, she was now.

Jason glanced at the kids in the other rooms. One. Two. Three. Four . . . Lou was number five. Lou had said that in her dreams, there were always five kids trapped in the dollhouse, and nothing she could do to help them. Now it looked like it was Jason's turn to figure out a way to save them.

There's safety in numbers, he thought. *Let's bring them together!*

Jason dragged his fingers along the roofline, flicking open the latch that kept the dollhouse shut, and then pulled the front half of the house toward himself. The hinges squealed. He flinched, hoping that the creatures out in the darkness weren't drawn by the noise.

When he looked inside, the kids had changed. With the house opened, they'd become stiff, lifeless figurines. Dolls in a dollhouse. Jason reached in and opened the door where his sister was hiding. *Oh, no. No, no, no . . .* Lou had turned into a tiny likeness of herself. Holding his breath, praying she would be okay, he scooped her carefully into his hand and held her up. A part of him was grateful she wasn't squirming around; another part wished she *was* fighting back. He placed her into the room with the girl with pigtail braids, standing them so that they'd face each other when they came to life again. *If* they came to life again . . . "It'll be okay, Lou," he whispered. "Trust me. This is for the best."

Closing the house, Jason clasped the latch near the roofline. But when he peeked through the windows, the girls were not where he'd left them. Lou had disappeared. Had she returned to the closet from which he'd taken her? The girl with the braids was still looking tentatively around in the bedroom with the indigo wallpaper. She didn't appear to notice his interference.

So I can't move them around myself, he thought. *They can't hear me. And Lou probably thinks I'm a giant monster who wants to eat her up.*

There must be another way.

The growling sound started up from in the house again, and Jason noticed a dark shape several rooms to the right of the one where Lou was hiding. It looked like a swirling mass of dark mist or smoke. Jason felt his face drain of blood, dizziness creeping in at the edges of his vision, but he couldn't faint now. Lou needed him more than ever. He lunged to unlock the latch at the roofline, but his fingers slipped as he tried to turn it. When he finally got a grip, the latch would not budge.

The black mist continued to drag itself along the hallway. Was it looking for his sister? Jason clutched at the corners of the house and tried to lift it. It was too unwieldy, too heavy. Grasping the dollhouse under the eaves, Jason used all of his strength to shake the house, back and forth, back and forth.

The thing screeched and spat, losing its focus.

Yes! Jason thought. *It's working.*

Unfortunately, the kids inside the dollhouse were scream-ing too.

Lou clutched at her knees as the closet rocked violently. Memories of the last earthquake back home rushed through her mind, and she covered her head with her hands. Were closets safe places? She couldn't remember. But she did know that setting herself underneath a doorway was supposed to help.

She swung the closet door open to find another girl stand-ing just on the other side. The girl wore denim overalls and her hair hung in two braids. Lou let out a yelp and nearly fell backward. Unfazed, the other girl grabbed her forearms and pulled Lou from the cramped space.

"I heard you shouting from down the hall," said the girl with the braids. "We've got to get out. Follow me." She took Lou's hand and they raced across the room with the bleeding marble busts and out through another door into a long, dark hallway.

The shaking grew more violent, and the two girls tumbled to the floor. Lou clutched at the girl's biceps and then clamped her eyes shut. "Please don't leave me," she whispered.

Eventually, the growling sound began to fade.

"I don't plan on it," said the girl, struggling to rise. Helping Lou to her feet, she added, "My name is Sadie. What's yours?"

It was working! The more Jason shook the house, the more the shadow thing faded. Just a little more. Just a little harder, and maybe it would go away completely.

Lou and the girl with the braids were in the hallway not far from where the mass was pulling at shadows, as if trying to rebuild itself. The two had fallen and were scrambling to stand.

Jason was about to jolt the dollhouse again when a pair of hands reached out of the darkness and steadied his own. He screamed and nearly toppled from the house's halo of light, but the hands grabbed his wrists and held him upright. "Shhh . . ."

From the other side of the dollhouse, a girl was staring at him. For a moment, there was a glint in her eyes, like flame from a candlewick. Though her dress was dark, her apron reflected the glow of the house, giving her an aura of warmth. She raised a finger to her lips. Jason tried to slow his breath.

He glanced through a window. Lou and the other girl had made their way into another room and were leaning against the door from inside.

Safe . . . for now.

"Lou," he said, his voice echoing into the dark.

"Shhh. It'll hear us," the girl in the black dress whispered. "And I really wouldn't recommend shaking the dollhouse again. You'll only make it angrier."

"It?" Jason lowered his voice too. "What is *it* exactly?"

The girl shook her head. "It doesn't know that I brought you here. Not yet anyway."

"*You* brought me here?" he asked.

She went on. "My name is Connie Caldwell, and once upon a time, this dollhouse belonged to me."

CHAPTER 6

"THIS THING WAS yours?" Jason asked. "But how?"

She raised her finger to her lips again, shook her head, and glanced worriedly out into the void. She was afraid of something hearing them.

But Lou's safety was at stake. "My sister, Louise, dreams about this dollhouse. That there are five kids trapped inside. A monster chases them. I'm pretty sure I just saw it!" Connie motioned wildly for him to keep quiet. Frustrated, Jason threw his hands in the air. "There's got to be something I can do to help her," he whispered. "You said you brought us here?"

"I brought *you* here," she said so quietly, he barely heard her. "Not the others."

"You must have done it for a reason. Right?"

Connie nodded slowly. She held out her hand. As he took it, she closed her eyes and exhaled slowly. Jason closed his eyes too, imitating the speed of Connie's long breath.

It felt like the atmosphere had changed, as if the atoms of the air were attempting to make him into something new. The feeling of pins and needles pressed into his skin. He reached out for the dollhouse's rooftop to steady himself, but found himself instead holding on to something cold and solid and unfamiliar.

Snapping open his eyes, he realized that they were standing inside a long room. At the far end, high shelves were filled with hundreds of books. Overhead, two chandeliers glowed dimly, their many crystals shivering and clinking. The group stood beside a carved marble fireplace.

Connie let go of his other hand. "There," she said. "It's safer to speak inside."

"How did you . . ." Jason trailed off. There was a large portrait on the wall over the fireplace mantel—a painting of Connie staring out from a glistening, carved gilt frame. Her blue eyes glimmered with sorrow.

Connie noticed where his gaze had strayed. "I've lived at Larkspur House for a long time. The dollhouse was based on the actual mansion." She paused, lost for a moment in her memories. "When this place reached out for your sister and the others, I knew I needed to bring you along to help her. She trusts you in a way that she'd never trust a stranger like me."

He shook his head, ashamed. "But I just scared her."

"That wasn't your fault. You didn't know."

Anger flushed through him. He wasn't mad at the girl exactly, but she was standing right there, and she was the easiest target. "I thought I was going crazy!" Connie only stared at him, waiting for him to calm down, as if she'd expected this reaction. He choked down what felt like venom before speaking again. "Now that we're inside, can you take me to Lou?"

"I can," said Connie, waving for him to follow her to the bookshelves. Hanging on the wall was a large mirror. She touched the glass. When her hand met her reflection, the image of a different room appeared in the mirror. "Let's go," she said, before stepping through the glass as if it were a door.

Jason raised his foot and slowly pushed into the mirror's surface. It felt like he was climbing into a pool of water, ripples tickling his skin. He closed his eyes and held his breath.

Now they were in a grand foyer. The ceiling arched high overhead, and a circular parquet pattern gleamed from the wooden floor. Connie approached a window in an adjacent room. Her reflection was just solid enough that she could touch it. She stepped through the glass again.

Again, Jason followed.

They went like this, from room to room, until finally, they entered a hall where Lou and Sadie were striding confidently in the opposite direction.

Relief made him dizzy. "Lou! Wait! It's me! I'm here!" he called out to his sister.

But Lou didn't turn back. The girls were talking to each other about the fastest route toward an exit.

"Lou!" he tried again.

Connie squeezed his shoulder. She shook her head and shushed him again. Annoyed, he pulled back and ran after his sister.

When he was several steps away, he reached out for Lou's hand. But his own hand bounced off, as if he and his sister were repelling magnets. She didn't flinch, didn't turn around, didn't notice at all.

Jason looked back to Connie. "What's wrong? Can't she—"

"Larkspur is a strange place," Connie whispered, hurrying after the girls. "You and I are . . . like ghosts here. If you want to communicate with your sister, you need to play by different rules."

"What rules?"

Connie crossed her arms. "Rule number one," she whispered. "Do not make the creature aware of you."

Lou and Sadie wandered off around a corner. Panic roiling in his gut, Jason called out again. "Lou!" Connie squeezed his shoulder again. Harder this time, enough that it hurt.

Down the hall, from the opposite direction, the growling sound came again. Now that he was inside the house, he could feel the floor vibrate and hear the walls and the ceiling creak.

Uh-oh . . .

Connie cleared her throat. When Jason turned to face her, she said, "This was a mistake. *I told you* . . ."

He blinked, and she was gone.

CHAPTER 7

"STRAIGHT AHEAD," **SAID** Lou, pointing toward a set of stairs. "There should be a door at the bottom."

The growling sound erupted behind them again.

The girls hurried forward. At the top of the staircase, they looked back to find the hallway was still empty.

"How do you know so much about this place?" asked Sadie.

Heat flooded Lou's face. She tried to put together the answer to Sadie's question in her head before she spoke it aloud, but every combination of words would make her sound insane. Finally, she just blurted it all out. "It looks almost exactly like my dollhouse back home."

She told Sadie about her nightmares and Marcus and what she'd overheard her mother and aunt talking about from the kitchen and then how she'd fallen asleep in Marcus's bed in Ohio before waking up on the velvet daybed in the room down the hall.

By the time they reached the bottom step, Sadie stared at her with relief. "I don't know how any of this happened, but I'm glad to have you with me, Louise."

Lou was shocked that this stranger seemed to accept everything that Lou had just told her. There was a *realness* in her eyes—something that the rest of this place was lacking. "It's Lou," she said with a shy smile. "And I'm glad we're together too, but I wish we didn't have to be. How did you . . . find yourself here?"

But Sadie wasn't looking at Lou anymore. They'd reached the door Lou had said would be there. Four panes of glass looked out on pitch darkness. Sadie grabbed the knob and attempted to turn it. "Locked!"

"Can I try?" Lou wriggled the knob for a few seconds before giving up. She leaned forward toward the glass, trying to block her own reflection, but she couldn't see anything. It was too dark outside.

"Should we break the glass?" Sadie asked.

Lou thought of the giant eyeball that had been staring in at her through the window upstairs and stepped back. "I'm not sure I want to go out there."

"We can't stay in here. We're not alone."

"What can we use to smash it?" Lou asked, her voice sounding weak and wobbly in her ears.

Sadie slipped her foot out of one of her big black boots. She picked it up. "This?"

Lou was unsure, but answered, "It looks solid enough."

"Watch out." Sadie swung the boot at the window. It bounced and fell to the floor with a sad thump. "Gosh. That's thick glass."

"Put your hand inside the boot and just . . . *punch*."

Sadie raised an eyebrow, impressed. "Is this something you've done before?"

The kids in Lou's dreams had tried many methods of escaping the house. But the windows in the dream version of her dollhouse had always been unbreakable. Lou shook her head. Sadie shoved her hand into the boot, but quickly pulled it out again. Cringing, she said, "I don't want to hurt myself. If I break a bone, I can't play my ukulele."

"Ukulele?" asked Lou.

Sadie leaned back and raised her eyebrows. She paused for a few seconds before asking, "Do I look familiar to you?"

Lou shook her head again. "I'm sorry. Should you?"

Sadie sighed as if relieved. "You're not Canadian, then."

41

Lou almost burst out laughing. "Um . . . I live in California with my family, just east of the Bay Area."

"I'm from Toronto. It's just me and my mom. She's my manager."

"Manager? For what?"

"I'm a singer."

"Oh, wow. That's so . . . cool!" It felt like a strange time to be impressed. "And you play the ukulele?"

Sadie nodded, but then her eyes glazed, as if a bit of life had left them. Lou could tell that bad memories were swimming in the girl's head. "I was on a Canadian Broadcasting talent show. I made it to the semifinals by performing my own version of 'Somewhere Over the Rainbow' from *The Wizard of Oz.*"

"Sadie!" Lou said, her excitement spilling out. "That's amazing!"

"It was only the semifinals. No biggie." She held out her hand.

"*Yes*, biggie," said Lou, but Sadie pressed her lips together and turned back to the door. "Here, let me try." Sadie handed her boot to Lou, but before Lou could stick her hand inside, she noticed movement in the window of the door. There was someone waving to her from the other side.

Lou jumped, then looked closer.

No, he wasn't on the other side. He was in the window. Behind her . . . It was a reflection! She spun to find the space totally empty. Turning back to the window, she noticed the shadowy boy mouthing her name.

She asked Sadie in a hushed voice, "Do you see him too?" Sadie nodded. Lou rubbed her dry tongue on the roof of her mouth. "He looks like my brother, Jason," Lou added. She watched in confusion as he waved more frantically and then jumped up and down. "I don't like this."

"You don't like your brother?"

"No . . . Not that. It's just . . . This is the second time I've seen him since I arrived. The first time—" *He was a giant, peeking in at me through the window upstairs.* Lou worried that Sadie might stop listening to her. "The first time I saw him, the house started trembling. I feel like I can't trust what I'm seeing. Something here is playing tricks on us."

Jason was shaking his head, as if he could hear what she was saying.

"Maybe it's not really your brother," Sadie said out of the side of her mouth. "Have you ever heard of a doppelgänger? An evil spirit that looks like a twin?"

The words were like an icy breeze blowing inside Lou's shirt. "Let's get away from the door. Find someplace safe to hide."

"Like that closet where I found you?"

"Maybe not *there*," said Lou, blushing. "Come on. This way. We'll find a different exit." Sadie put her boot back on, but left the laces untied. Lou gave one last fearful glance at the boy in the window before she rushed away, trembling.

They made their way to an alcove in the hallway, where the exterior wall bowed outward, forming a rotunda-like space. A pair of high-backed chairs sat next to several windows covered by thick amber-colored curtains. The girls pulled the chairs farther into the rotunda, out of sight from anyone who might be searching the hallway, and then they sat down. "Are we safe here?" Sadie asked, peering toward the hallway.

"For the moment."

"Do you recognize where we are? According to your dollhouse?"

Lou sighed and shook her head. "Parts of it match the layout exactly. And then I'll turn a corner, and it's like someone added on another huge section of the house. I don't know if I'll be able to find another way out."

"Yes, you will," said Sadie. "Just pay attention to what looks familiar. If I ever lose my focus while playing music, I just think back to the song's chorus and then start again from there. Most times, my brain will reset, and I'll be able to keep going."

Lou pressed her lips together and nodded.

Sadie leaned closer and whispered, "I think it was a song that brought me here."

"A song brought you here?" Lou echoed. "How?"

Sadie blinked and bit her lip. "When I was on the talent show, the judges loved me. And the audience kept voting for me to continue. Then, during my last live performance, something weird happened. My ukulele kept going out of tune. I asked if I could start over. I was sooo nervous. I played the intro again, but after a few notes, the strings snapped."

"Oh my goodness!"

"They hit me in the face, cutting my cheek and scratching my cornea."

Lou wished she could hug the girl, but Sadie looked stiff, like she didn't want to be touched.

"I had to leave the show. And by the time I recovered, they'd already crowned a winner. He deserved it, I guess. But I swore I'd never play that ukulele again. My mom was furious, because she thought I was throwing away my future, but also, her own mom had given me the ukulele as a gift. It was an antique and very expensive."

"But it hurt you. So that's understandable."

"Is it?" Sadie asked. "For months I had a feeling that the ukulele itself wanted me to fail. But inanimate objects don't have feelings. Do they?"

Lou thought of her dollhouse and wasn't sure how to answer.

"Anyway, I shut the ukulele up in its case and put it in my closet. Then, earlier this month, a song kept getting stuck in my head. It was something that I don't remember ever hearing before. But I'd wake up in the morning with it already running through my mind, over and over. It was driving me crazy. I finally went online to look up ways to make it stop. One site recommended just playing the song until it goes away. I couldn't think of anything better, so I grabbed my ukulele and sat down to figure out the notes." Sadie paused, trying to catch her breath. "The next thing I knew, I was sitting in an unfamiliar room. My ukulele was gone. I was so sleepy, I could barely keep my head up. I felt like I'd just woken from a bad dream. I went off exploring, and a few minutes later, the house began to shake. And then . . . I found you."

Lou trembled. "You think your ukulele had something to do with this?"

"It sounds silly. But . . . yeah. I do. I knew what happened at the talent show was the instrument's fault. I thought I'd give anything to find my confidence again, to keep playing my music. But not like this. This is . . . *scary*."

"Agreed," said Lou. "I . . . something similar happened with my dollhouse. I started sleepwalking and having nightmares, and I just knew that it was the dollhouse causing it. When my parents tried to get rid of it, it came back. Like magic."

Sadie's brow scrunched up in disbelief.

From down the hallway there came the muffled sounds of screaming.

The girls stood and grabbed each other's hands.

"Someone else is in the house," said Lou.

"What if it's another trick? Like the image of your brother in the window?"

"You came looking for me when I was freaking out in the closet. What if this is another kid who needs help? What if they're hurt?"

CHAPTER 8

AS LOU AND Sadie crept down the hallway, the screaming grew louder, more panicked. It was coming from behind a closed door. When Lou reached for the knob, Sadie gave her a look that asked if she was *sure*. Lou nodded and pushed the door inward.

Light was flickering from overhead. The sound of a small motor clicked and shuddered. On the far wall, red curtains hung from either side of a large screen. A movie was playing. In it, children were running through dense woods, pursued by someone in a fake-looking monster costume with an enormous papier-mâché mask with giant yellow bug-like eyes and thick fang-tusks that came straight out of its mouth. The movie looked like it had been shot on a phone camera.

The screaming the girls had heard was coming from speakers embedded in the walls.

Several rows of seats faced the screen. Gold-painted plaster cherubs decorated the edges of the screen and clung to the walls in bas-relief, as if their playtime had been frozen.

"This is weird," said Sadie. "I don't want to be in here."

Just then, a blond boy sat up from one of the seats and turned toward them. The girls jumped in surprise, but then the boy held up his hands in apology. "I didn't hear you come in. Sorry to scare you!" He stood and came over, extending his hand. "I'm Cal." He motioned over his shoulder. "And this is my movie."

"*Your* movie," said Lou, unable to control her sudden scowl. "What does that mean?"

"I made it! Well, me and a group of my friends here in Greencliffe made it. But I wrote the script and directed it."

"Did you say Greencliffe?" Lou asked. Cal nodded. "Weird. That's the town where my mom's family grew up. New York, right?"

"Well . . . *yeah*." Cal looked confused. "That's where we are right now."

Lou shook her head. "As strange as it sounds, I'm not sure we're *anywhere* right now." She held out her hand. "I'm Lou. I live in California."

"Sadie," said Sadie, keeping her hands to herself. "Toronto." The girls explained how they'd ended up here—Lou waking inside a giant version of her dollhouse and Sadie's ukulele sending her into some sort of trance.

Now Cal looked shocked. "In Greencliffe, there are these ruins of an old mansion called Larkspur House. Everyone from my town knows the legends. The place is super-*duper* haunted. They say that every few years, a group of kids goes missing up at the site. There're tons of articles about the disappearances online. But I think the ruins are inspiring. In fact, it's where my friends and I filmed most of my movie. Of course, I had to *beg* them to come with me." He glanced at the screen, where the green monster was using a single claw to pin a boy against a tree trunk, then he looked back at Lou. "You think this place looks like your old dollhouse?"

Lou nodded, unsure where he was going with this.

"I'm pretty sure that this house *is* Larkspur. Or at least it's how Larkspur used to look, before it burned down."

"If it burned down," Sadie began, "then how are we standing inside it?"

Cal shrugged. "All I know is that earlier today, I came back to do more scouting for the final scenes of my movie." Giddiness shone in his eyes. "When I stepped across the old stone foundation, it was like the ruins had turned back up into a house! I mean . . . *Hello!*" He threw his hands in the air. "The walls and floors were solid. They looked brand-new! I had to pinch myself to make sure that I wasn't dreaming. If I *am*, it's a dream come true."

"So then, this place is Larkspur House," said Lou. Her mind churned, thinking about her mom and aunt's conversation. "Since my mom and aunt grew up in Greencliffe, they must have known about the mansion. And all these years later, my cousin disappears around here trying to get to a music academy."

Cal scowled. "There is no music academy in Greencliffe. Larkspur was once home to an artist and his family, and later, it became an orphanage where a whole bunch of kids died in a fire."

Lou's fingers felt numb. The nightmares that had tormented her for the past few months were starting to make sense. Kids trapped in a house, pursued by a monster made of shadow. Or maybe . . . *smoke*.

"And you went there?" Sadie asked Cal. "On purpose?"

"I didn't think anything bad would happen to me."

"What do you think now?" Sadie gestured to the room in which they were standing.

"This isn't *bad*," said Cal. "This is amazing! I have no clue how it's happening, but I know for sure that I'll be able to work it into my movie eventually."

"We tried looking for an exit," said Lou. "But the door was locked. And I think the windows are un-smashable."

"Why would you want to leave yet?"

"Because there's something here. Something evil. It growls and shakes the floor and the walls and the ceiling. And it's been chasing us. Haven't you noticed?"

"Nope." Cal shook his head, amused. "I've been in this room. Enjoying the dark. Seeing my movie on a big screen is amazing."

The puzzle of this day kept rearranging inside Lou's head. She was desperate to figure out what was going on. Cal had just provided a bunch more pieces, which made the picture even bigger, more complex. If they could learn what was happening, there was a better chance that they could stop it. "What if we're inside the ghost of Larkspur House?"

Sadie crossed her arms, as if Lou's theory had made her chilly. "Do houses *have* ghosts? I don't mean just *other people's* ghosts. Like, ghosts of *themselves*?"

"Doesn't it seem like something that could happen in a horror movie?" Lou asked. "A mysterious force lures some kids into a creepy old house?"

Cal's face lit up. "Ooh," he said, his voice low. "Maybe that's what this is: We're *in* a horror movie!"

Lou raised an eyebrow. "I didn't mean *literally*. Do you think that sounds more likely than what I suggested about the ghost of the house?"

"We need to find out what's going on," said Sadie. "How'd we get here? I hate the not knowing."

"What's it matter?" asked Cal. "Whenever you're ready, we'll just walk out the front door."

Lou squinted at him. She didn't like how he felt he knew all the answers. "I told you we already tried that," she said, thinking of the five kids trapped in her dreams. "Besides, if this *is* like a horror move, as you seem to wish, do you really think the villain would let us go so easily?"

Cal rolled his eyes.

"So then what do we do?" Sadie asked.

"I still remember parts of my dollhouse's floor plan. Granted, these halls aren't exactly the same, but they're close enough. If the doors are locked and the windows are unbreakable, we head for an exit where there aren't any doors or windows."

"Such as?"

Lou cleared her throat. "A chimney." The smile that appeared on Sadie's face made Lou feel like she was onto something.

"You want us to crawl up a chimney?" said Cal. "Like Santa Claus? Do you know how difficult that is?"

"Not really," Lou answered. Half joking, she added, "My family doesn't celebrate Christmas."

Cal considered this. "Fair enough," he said, nodding.

Sadie gasped and then nudged Lou toward the movie screen on the wall.

When Lou saw Jason staring at them from inside the screen, her insides turned to gelatin.

CHAPTER 9

"WHO'S THAT?" CAL asked, staring at the screen. "He's not part of my movie."

"It's my brother," Lou whispered. "I think . . . whatever brought all of us here is using his image to scare me."

"Are you usually scared of your brother?"

"No. I love Jason . . . most of the time." Lou backed toward the doorway where she and Sadie had entered the screening room. "It's like this house, or something in it, is trying to get inside my head. To warp my thoughts and my memories. To turn good things into bad things. If it really *is* him, I'm terrified he'll leave me by myself."

Jason stared at her and shook his head. Lou couldn't look away from the screen. He was moving his mouth but all that was coming out of the speakers were the screaming sounds from Cal's film. The horror-movie characters continued to run around in the background, unaware that Jason had moved into the center. Lou tried to make out what her brother was trying to say from the shape of his lips. *Help me, please.* Or it could be *It's me, Lou. It's really me.*

Jason's eyes suddenly lit up, glowing a deep and fiery amber. The sound from Cal's film started to cut out, and a growling noise took its place, coming through the speakers so loudly that the three of them had to cover their ears to block it out. Lou's skin prickled. Now she was sure this was not her brother.

His eyes drew back, sinking deep into his skull. His nose and mouth protruded outward until he looked more like a goat or a horse. A monstrous, *giant* horse. His white skin grew thin and translucent and as it stretched, Lou could see bones and muscles moving underneath. The thing's shoulders expanded into sharp points, and Jason's shirt ripped away, exposing a torso that appeared to be made of tree roots and bramble vines.

Even worse, however, was his smile—wide and cruel and ravenous—crammed with huge teeth and sharp, misshapen shards of bone.

"Wow!" said Cal, his jaw agape. "That is *so* cool. I wish I could do effects like that!"

"Jason, please!" Lou shouted at the screen. "Stop! You're scaring me."

The thing opened its mouth and whispered in a drawn-out, rough-hewn whisper, "*Goooooooood.*"

A black mist seemed to be moving around inside the creature's body, seeping out of cracks and fissures every few seconds, twisting into little curls before disappearing. Lou understood suddenly that this was the shadow thing that always chased the five kids through the dollhouse in her dreams. It had stolen away her brother's face, and now it would chase her too.

"Don't be scared," Cal said to Lou. "It's only a movie. It can't hurt you."

As if to prove him wrong, an amber glow lit inside the eyes of the little plaster cherubs that decorated the room. Their chubby faces turned and glared at Lou and Sadie and Cal, who looked back in awe. All at once, the sculptures leapt out from their bas-reliefs, off the walls, crawling away from the carved armrests of the theater seats.

They darted about near the ceiling—their eyes like lightning bugs on a hot summer night—beating their angelic wings furiously. Then the little beasts bolted down, swiping at the kids' faces.

Cal ducked and screamed, as if finally understanding that this wasn't a game.

Pain scratched across Lou's forehead. One of the cherubs was hovering before her. It furrowed its brow and drew back its lips, revealing needle-sharp fangs.

Without thinking, Lou punched it. The cherub went flying. It hit against a wall, breaking off its plaster wings and falling lifeless to the floor. Sadie swung out her arms as the creatures swooped at her, bashing several at a time. With each hit, the lights went out of their eyes. A couple of cherubs grabbed at Lou's hair, yanking her head back and forth so fiercely that she couldn't get a sense of where they were. Several more came at her face, raking their nails across her cheeks. Cal hopped up and leapt over a couple of seats toward the girls. Lightning fast, he gripped the cherubs that were attacking Lou and threw them to the ground, stomping their plaster bodies until they were dust. Lou knocked a few more away and then stomped on them too. "Thank you," she cried.

"I'm so sorry," Cal choked out. "I didn't realize—"

The bone-thing on the movie screen spat out what might have been laughter. Black mist oozed from its snout and swirled out into the light from the projector, mixing with the galaxies of dust particles.

"You can apologize later," yelled Sadie. "Let's get out of here *now*!" She bolted up the aisle that rose toward the door at the back of the room.

But Lou couldn't tear her gaze away from the movie screen. The creature leaned out toward the camera. Then it reached for her. Broken talons met the fourth wall. The screen stretched outward like plastic wrap, and its arms emerged into the screening room. They came quickly, fingers wriggling with excitement as they careened toward Lou and Cal.

"Come on!" Sadie shrieked, opening the door.

Lou snapped back into her body. She grabbed Cal's wrist and pulled him along the aisle, toward the ramp. Looking over her shoulder, she noticed the creature's snout pushing out of the movie screen. In moments, the giant creature would be in the screening room with them.

Sadie held the door as they rushed past her, then slammed it shut.

CHAPTER 10

WHAT HAD HAPPENED was this: Jason had been stepping through the house's mirrors like Connie had shown him, until, peering out through the projector lens in the screening room, he'd found Lou chatting with a couple of other kids. "Lou!" he shouted out, trying to get her attention. *"It's me! It's me! It's me!"*

Then she turned. She saw him. For a brief moment, something lit in her eyes, as if she finally understood. He was *here*. But he could feel the creature close by.

He needed to tell them to run. Now.

He felt a shifting inside himself, as if a small animal were crawling through his guts. Panic set in as he imagined a creature moving his liver out of the way, pressing past his lungs as it came upward, slithering up his esophagus into his throat and into his sinuses. He tried to focus on his sister, tried to open his mouth to warn her, but his jaw froze. Suddenly, his eyes were on fire. The image of the screening room blurred, then black smoke churned into his vision, and he couldn't see anything anymore.

The creature had found him, just like Connie had said it would, and it was pushing him out of the way. Stopping him from speaking to these kids. He tried to shout out to Lou, but before a scream could burst from his throat, he was flying through darkness, unable to see which way was up. He flailed his arms and legs. Any second he might hit the bottom of a bottomless pit. *SPLAT.* Instead, he found himself tumbling and bouncing across scorched ground—the way a stone will skip upon the surface of a lake—until he skidded to a stop in the middle of a black nothingness.

He was in the void again. Connie's warning had come true. He'd only wanted to warn Lou, but he'd led the creature straight to her. His eyes stung, and he felt like a fool. "Lou," he whispered. "No. Please, I hope you ran . . ."

He sat up, ignoring the warm wetness that was dripping from his scraped knees and elbows and his chin. His whole body ached. What felt most damaged was his mind; he couldn't escape the look on his sister's face when he'd appeared on the movie screen. She'd been terrified. He'd heard her say that she didn't trust what she'd seen in that house, which meant that she didn't trust *him*. Maybe Connie would have a better idea how to get through.

Connie.

Jason sighed. He'd messed up. Shouting, screaming, bringing attention to himself. To his sister! Even if he were able to locate her, would Connie even want to help anymore? The only way to find out was to make his way back to the dollhouse and ask her.

He looked around, but the pinpoint of light that had previously been his beacon was nowhere to be seen. His lungs clenched at the thought of being lost out here, and he fought for breath. Was it possible to feel dizzy when there wasn't even enough light available to see the earth slope beneath you? He tried to stand, but he stumbled forward. Yes. It was possible.

His bare foot crunched on something that felt like a dry stick. But when the stick screeched and scrambled away, Jason remembered how *not* alone he was out here. He pricked up his ears and inched his feet forward, hoping that his path was clear. He couldn't imagine stepping on something that might wish to crush him in return.

Which way? Which way? Which way?

"I don't know what to do," he whispered. "I'm sorry, Louise. I'm so, so sorry."

Something in the distance caught his eye. It wasn't the glow from inside the dollhouse, but another kind of light. Dim and pale and stretching along a line that cut through the void like silver pen on black paper. Someone was standing within this light—a dark figure—staring in his direction. Jason crouched down, hoping the shadows were like a dark cloak and that whoever it was hadn't spotted him.

CHAPTER 11

CLAMORING DOWN THE hallway, Lou, Sadie, and Cal had almost made it back to the rotunda alcove when they realized that the thing from the movie screen wasn't following them.

"Is everyone okay?" Cal asked, his chest heaving.

Lou's scalp ached where the plaster cherubs had yanked her hair, and her cheeks stung were they'd scratched her. Other than that—

"Fine," she whispered. Sadie just nodded, as if she were only partially present.

"What just happened?" Cal went on. "That creature . . ."

"It's what I told you was after us," said Lou. "Remember? The growling. The trembling floors and walls. The thing from my nightmares."

"You said something earlier about floor plans," Sadie managed to whisper. Shaking away her fear, she added, "And a chimney?"

"My dollhouse had several. I'll just need to figure out exactly where we are right now. There must be something I recognize nearby."

"What about this?" Cal led them to a railing on the right side of the hall. It overlooked a wide dark room with no windows.

Glancing up, Lou noticed that the ceiling was made of glass. Strips of iron crisscrossed over rows of girders, holding up the panes in a slight arch. Beyond, the sky was so black, it almost looked as though there were a big tent pitched overhead. Below was a shiny floor that looked like an enormous mirror made of onyx.

"Perfect!" she said. "It's the indoor pool. I used to pour water inside here when the dollhouse was small enough to take only a few cupfuls. There should be another room at the far end with a fireplace inside."

"But how do we get down?" asked Sadie. "There aren't any stairs."

"We climb down?"

Lou went first, swinging one leg over, then the other. Sadie held Lou's arms through the rungs as Lou lowered herself past the edge of the balcony. She dangled for several seconds before dropping to the tiled floor below with a hard thump. Sadie and Cal followed. "This way." Lou led them around the left side of the pool. Huge potted plants made the edges of the room feel like a jungle. To their right, the water looked as solid as polished stone.

The only light came from the hallway where they'd climbed down. "Don't get too close to the edge," Sadie said to Cal as he peered over the side of the pool.

Lou wondered if she'd see her brother's reflection looking back up at her if she peeked in, so she stayed far from the water. Their footfalls echoed around the room. She crossed her fingers, praying silently that the door she expected to find would be there.

When her palm closed around the doorknob, she nearly yelped with glee, but she kept her lips sealed. "Found it," she told the others calmly.

When she pushed the door inward, she saw an orange light flickering in the new room. Bad news. She cringed, then hung her head.

Stepping aside, she showed Sadie and Cal why she was disappointed. Inside the wide mouth of the fireplace in the corner of the room, a fire engulfed a pyramid of thick logs. On the stone mantel, more flames danced at the wicks of red taper candles.

"*Crud*," said Cal, stepping inside and closing the door behind him.

"Is someone here?" asked Sadie, her eyes flicking around to the darker parts of the room. "Someone who set the fire?"

But Lou had already checked. She shook her head. "The house knew what we were trying to do. It found a way to stop us."

"The house can *start fires*?" Cal asked, wearing a worried look.

Lou noticed a claw-foot bathtub several yards from the fireplace. "Luckily, we know how to put out fires," Lou answered. She twisted the handle by the bathtub faucet, but the pipes merely rattled and clanged. No water spilled out.

"*Stop, stop, stop!*" Sadie whispered at the sound. "That thing from the screening room will know where to find us."

"Sorry," said Lou, stepping back.

"We could just wait for the fire to go out," said Cal.

"Not now, we can't," Sadie answered. "The creature could be coming straight for us."

Lou crossed her arms. "Don't you think if it was going to chase us, it would already have come?"

Cal stepped in front of Sadie. "Do you have another suggestion?"

Sadie straightened her spine and glared at him. "Well, there *is* a pool filled with gallons of water on the other side of that door. We could dump out one of the potted plants and fill up the empty container to douse the flames in here."

Cal stared back. After a moment, he muttered, "That's a great idea, actually." Then he held up his hand for a high five. Sadie scoffed and walked away, following Lou to the door that led to the pool.

The pool room was so dark, her eyes needed time to adjust. But her nose worked perfectly well, and the aroma that was now filling the space was like a mixture of churned earth and wet asphalt. Lou winced.

"What is that smell?" Cal asked.

Lou crept forward. The light from the flames behind her revealed that the lip of the pool dropped down into nothingness. The slick black surface of the water had vanished. "How?" she whispered. "It was *just* full."

"Don't get too close," Sadie said, grabbing her elbow.

Now that the pool had no water, the three could see that the bottom was filled with other things. A rusted old-fashioned wheelchair was turned onto its side. Nearby was a half-rotted wicker bassinet, and beside that was a wire crate that looked like it had once transported chickens or tiny dogs. Several pale faces stared up from the mess—cracked doll heads and plastic animal masks. There was even a very small desk and chair that looked like they should have been in a kindergarten classroom. Scattered all around were broken frames that held blackened and torn up paintings. The pictures were so badly ruined, Lou couldn't make out the images they'd once contained.

Coating the bottom of the pool was a thick, black sludge, in which all these objects were stuck.

Breaking the silence, Sadie asked, "Why are those things down there?" Cal and Lou didn't have a chance to answer.

The door behind them slammed shut, leaving them in darkness.

CHAPTER 12

THE FIGURE IN the distance raised a hand, and Jason squeezed his knees to his chest, choking down nausea. It had seen him!

It waved at him slowly. Was it friendly? Or was this a trap? Twinges of hurt echoed through Jason's body where the creature had invaded him. He wouldn't go through something like that again. Maybe it was better to just hide until the figure had passed by. He slid himself backward, away from the faint light of the path.

Pain bloomed across his skin as claws raked down his spine. Jason scrambled to his feet. He clamped his hand over his mouth as he turned around. In the shadows, he saw the dim outline of an immense, insectile creature. Rancid breath misted into Jason's face, and he felt his body go numb. The thing chittered and then darted forward. Instinct yanked Jason back before the creature could make contact again. He dashed in the opposite direction, the thing scraping the ground behind him. The waving figure didn't seem so bad anymore.

As he careened closer to the path of light, the sounds of the creature faded behind him.

He ran and ran. The waving figure held its arms open, as if in comfort. Closer now, Jason slowed.

The person on the path was wearing a floor-length black dress, cinched at the waist. A dark cape fell from the shoulders, and a hood was pulled up over long hair. A pale face was partially obscured by a transparent black veil.

When he'd come within a dozen feet, Jason saw that she was a woman. She stopped waving and called out to him, "Quiet, now. They'll hear you." Jason didn't like the word *they*. He clapped his bare arms across his belly and hunched his sore spine, as if that might protect him from another swipe. The voice sounded high-pitched, yet crinkly and worn, as if it hadn't been in use for quite some time. "We never stray from the path," she went on, calmly, sweetly. "Most of the things in the dark won't venture into the light, no matter how faint." She arced her arm to indicate the line of silvery phosphorescence stretching in both directions, then nodded. "What were you doing all the way out there?"

"I-I didn't listen to someone who was trying to help me," he said, his breath shaking his rib cage. "I-I messed up. And I . . . e-ended up out h-here." Shivering, he added, "I need to find my sister."

Through the veil, Jason saw the woman smile sadly. "The house has her?" she asked.

He nodded, fighting tears.

"A shame," she said. "It's a hungry place. Never satisfied."

"Who . . . who are you?"

"Ah!" came a pip of an exclamation, as if she'd realized suddenly that they hadn't been introduced. "We do not share names on this road. Dangerous. However, for simplicity's sake, you may call me Madame. What should I call you?"

No names? Jason thought for a moment before answering. "Brother . . . I guess."

She tilted her head, taking in his word. Nodding, she added, "*Brother* it shall be."

"Do you know which way leads back to the house?" he asked.

The veiled woman blinked and sighed. Jason somehow understood that she dreaded this question. She waved for him to follow her along the faded path.

"Can you tell me more about the house?"

"I can," she replied as she strolled with him. "But should I?" Jason wished she'd walk faster—who knew what was happening to Lou at the moment? "If you learned everything there is to know about Larkspur, you'd turn around and step lively in the opposite direction, whether you'd gathered up your sister or not."

This only made Jason want to know more. "Did you live there?"

"I was a visitor. I spent one afternoon at the house with my children. Larkspur made certain that I could never return . . ."

Footsteps were scuffling behind them. Looking back, Jason realized that they weren't alone. A line of stragglers appeared to be following them. Madame noticed and said, "Don't mind them. They're like me. A little lost. A touch forgotten." Jason paused to look at them. Several yards back was someone wearing an old-fashioned circus clown costume. There was a woman in a red dress suit and a tall man standing beside her, his hair slicked into a sharp part. And a woman in a black-and-white maid's uniform. And more, fading into the shadow farther along the path. "Most of all, they're curious about you. We all want you to succeed."

"Succeed?"

"The house is vulnerable at the moment. Over the decades, it's found many young victims. It works magic to frighten them, and their fear is what it feeds on. Fear replenishes it, helps it rebuild itself, fortifies its defenses, giving life to the evil within."

"That is . . . *horrifying*."

"If it has your sister, it will try to destroy her. I don't tell you this to frighten you. I want you to understand what is at stake. If the house succeeds, it will heal itself. It will continue to do the same to others. But if it fails now . . . well . . . it might actually fail forever."

Jason didn't need to hear more. "We'd better hurry. How much farther?"

The woman looked down at him, the whites of her eyes standing out against her dark makeup. "Farther than you'd like."

CHAPTER 13

STANDING IN THE darkness at the edge of the pool, Lou gasped. She ran to the room with the fireplace. It was much dimmer now. The tapers continued to glow from atop the mantel, but the fireplace itself had disappeared below, sealed up by a panel of bricks.

The fire that had been blocking the way was gone. And so was their exit.

"No!" Lou yelled. "It's not fair!"

"It can change shape," Sadie said to herself. "The freaking house can *change shape*."

"It's like the house is trying to keep us afraid," said Lou. "Keep us on our toes."

"Yes!" said Cal, his eyes big and glassy. "Just like in a horror movie."

"Make sure you take notes," Sadie told him, wearing a disgusted half smile, "in case we ever get out of here. Cool detail for a script."

A strange delight spread across Cal's face. "I won't forget any of this. Trust me."

"*Cal*," Lou said harshly, trying to capture his attention. "This isn't fun for us. Please."

"Oh, I know that. For real. No joke." In the candlelight, Lou watched his pink cheeks turn pinker. He put his hands on his hips, as if that might make him look more serious. "Is there another fireplace nearby? Another chimney?"

"I think so," Lou answered. She nodded at the door to the pool. "Back out that way. In a separate wing."

"What are we waiting for?" Sadie barreled past Cal.

Once they were in the pool room again, the candlelight winked out behind them. The illumination from the balcony across the way led them forward.

"Look!" said Cal, pointing at the pool. The water had returned, blacker and shinier than before.

"Wasn't this pool just empty?" Sadie asked. "Or am I going crazy?"

"If you're crazy," Lou said, "then we all are."

Sadie's jaw dropped. "Is that supposed to make me feel better?"

Lou thought of creeping into Jason's bedroom late at night, after a dream of the dollhouse. "Maybe? I tend to feel better when I know I'm not going through something all by myself."

"Why can't we find our way home?" Sadie's lip quivered. "I wish . . . I wish I had my ukulele. I wish I could play it again."

"We'll get you home," said Lou. "I promise."

"Don't promise anything," Sadie answered, her face turned stony. "Not here."

A splash came from the center of the pool.

They all scattered from the edge.

Small ripples spread out wider and wider. Lou scanned the surface but didn't notice anything that could have caused the disturbance.

Below the balcony railing, an archway opened into a dim hall.

"In a horror movie," Cal whispered, staring at the spreading ripples in the water, "this would be the part where we run."

He nudged the girls forward, and they took off, racing across the slick tile floor toward the dark archway.

Movement churned the water beside them, as if something large were propelling itself alongside them. Lou's eyes stung: She worried that if she didn't push herself, something horrifying would emerge from the pool, reach out, and pull her under. Water splashed out, soaking her legs, and she released a shriek that echoed around the space.

Seconds later, they huddled inside the new doorway, far from the edge of the pool. The water was motionless now. Not a ripple disturbed its surface. It was as if they'd all imagined it.

Lou pressed herself against the wall, unsure which was more frightening: knowing that something had chased them and was now hiding, or the idea that it had been in her head.

CHAPTER 14

AFTER WALKING FOR what might have been twenty hours—or maybe twenty minutes—Jason noticed the familiar pinpoint of orange light far off in the distance.

He turned to thank the veiled woman, but she was no longer strolling beside him. Glancing over his shoulder, he noticed only dim shadows of the crowd he'd seen earlier. Their footsteps continued to crunch along the path, which was enough to keep Jason moving onward.

By the time the dollhouse was near enough that he could make out its gables and spires and towers, the sounds of the people who'd accompanied him had died away. He whispered thank you to their shadows. He hated to think what might have happened to him if Madame hadn't waved to him.

Coming closer to the house, he listened for voices from within. He needed to know that his sister was okay. But all was silent.

A figure rose up from behind the dollhouse. Jason froze, imagining the insect thing that had scratched at his back. Then his eyes adjusted, allowing him to see Connie's disappointed face, and his muscles melted in relief.

He wanted to shout at her, *Why did you leave me alone?* But he already knew the answer and shouting again now might only drive her away. She'd left him alone because he hadn't listened to her warning.

"You made it," Connie whispered. Her voice was so quiet, Jason had to stare at her lips to be sure of what she was saying. Looking out at the darkness beyond the dollhouse, he searched for movement of large, gnarly silhouettes. He was too frightened to speak, but he had so much to ask. He nodded, unsure if it was the right time to open his mouth.

Peeking through the windows of the house, he noticed Lou wandering another dark hallway with the girl with braids and a blond boy. Lou glanced over her shoulder every few steps. "If you want to help these kids," Connie went on, "we need to be more cautious. The creature inside is sly. It'll stop at nothing to get what it wants. And what it wants more than anything is to—"

"To eat," Jason finished, his voice little more than a creaking in his throat. "It feeds on fear. I'm not sure *how*, but it's what Madame told me." Connie threw him a curious stare. "A woman in a black dress and a veil over her face." A spark of recognition lit in her eyes.

"So Dagmar is still out there," she said to herself. "Wandering."

"There were others too. I think . . . I think they might have been ghosts."

Connie made her eyes go wide. "*Ghosts?*" she echoed, a smile on her lips. "Sounds scary."

Jason shook his head. "They helped me. I would have ended up lost if I hadn't met them." Connie only nodded. "We've got to go back inside. My sister needs to know not to be scared. I tried to talk to her through the movie screen, but she took it the wrong way. She didn't see me. She saw the *monster*. I need to get her to trust me again so she'll listen."

Connie nodded again. "A difficult task. However, there are others in the house who your sister hasn't encountered yet." She pointed at the two figures who were in an upper part of the house. One was the boy with the round face and black cowboy shirt. The other was the girl with the polka-dot rockabilly dress. The two appeared to be having a disagreement.

The girl's arms were crossed, and she wouldn't face the boy, no matter how many times he circled her and tried to capture her attention. "Get *them* to trust you. Bring them to your sister's group. They could help you win her favor."

"I still won't be able to *talk* to them," said Jason. "How am I supposed to—"

Connie cut him off. "There are ways. I'll show you." She held out her hand again.

"You don't think I'm a . . . a *mistake* anymore?" he asked.

Connie considered him. "You've learned your lesson," she whispered with a small grin.

She clasped his fingers, and they were suddenly back inside the dollhouse. Jason didn't recognize the room. Why hadn't Connie brought him directly to the pair of kids they had just been watching?

She must have noticed his concern, because she whispered, "There are some things you should know before we go any further. Things about the house. And things about me." Jason found himself frozen, afraid of what she might say next. "Don't worry. It's nothing bad. Just . . . a bit of information that might prove useful to you."

"You already told me the dollhouse used to be yours." Jason raised an eyebrow. "But that must have been . . . ages ago."

"Ages?" Connie sniffed. "I suppose it was. Larkspur House was once a grand residence of the Hudson Valley. My father commissioned one of his friends from New York City to build a dollhouse replica of the estate. He gave it to me after my baby brother was born. I loved the dollhouse with all my heart. For a long while, I'd seen and heard things inside the *real* Larkspur that I couldn't explain. Things that frightened me and Mother. Things that would make Cyrus cry uncontrollably in his cradle.

"Playing with the dollhouse helped me escape from my fears. I would have rather lived there than in my own bedroom. I played with the house every day until . . . until I couldn't play with it anymore."

"Why couldn't you play with it anymore?" Jason asked. "Did someone steal it? Is that how it ended up at my mom's house in Greencliffe?"

Connie blinked, unable to look at him. "A fire broke out in my brother's nursery. It quickly spread through much of the manor. My brother and father survived. But Mother and I . . . We did not."

Jason flinched. "You mean . . ."

"I am not *alive*." Connie shifted her weight from foot to foot. Jason blinked slowly. It seemed so obvious now. "Please don't think I'm a monster," she implored.

"I don't think that," Jason managed to choke out.

"Most of the ghosts I know have no quarrel with the living. I still think of myself only as a girl. A girl who's learned many tricks in order to stick around this horrible place.

"You see, the thing that lurks here has haunted Larkspur for a long time. It's tried to banish me over the years, but how can I leave when I know that it lures children? That it scares them so badly they cannot help but become a part of it, like little minions. I won't rest until I know that the *evil* is put down."

Connie stared into Jason's eyes. "After the previous five children, I thought it would be over. I believed we'd defeated it. But somehow, the creature—*the house itself*—is still clinging to life."

"That's what Madame said back on the path."

"If we can find a way to help these new victims escape, the creature will have nothing else to feed on. This could finally mean the end of Larkspur. And I would be free to move on and join Mother, wherever her spirit has traveled."

"I'll help you however I can," he whispered. "I promise."

"Thank you, Jason. That's sweet of you." Her expression grew grim, her mouth pursed, her cheeks drained of color.

"I'm not sure exactly how the shadow creature was able to lure these new victims into this darker version—this *dream* version—of itself. But I have a feeling that if we can figure out the answer, we might also learn how to help them escape. That's why you must get your sister to see you as yourself. This boy and this girl might be able to help with that. You'll convince them that we mean well. Then we'll lead them to the other three, and they'll convince your sister too."

Jason nodded, thinking of home, of their parents fighting. He imagined the possibility that everything was so fragile, their family might simply fall to pieces. Impossible to reorganize and reassemble. "Lou needs to know that we're in this together."

"Very good," said Connie, a glint in her eye. "Now, let's go contact the others."

CHAPTER 15

"WHICH WAY?" SADIE asked. She was waiting with Lou and Cal near a fork in the hall. One short path was well lit by glass wall sconces. At the end was a closed door with a brass knob that glistened. The other path stretched far into shadow.

Lou shook her head. "This doesn't look familiar. I don't think this hallway was in my dollhouse. There should be another chimney just off the main foyer. But I have no clue how to get there from here."

Sadie stepped into the center of the passage, away from the walls like she was afraid that they might reach out and grab her. "Did the house change shape again?"

"Maybe," said Lou. "Or maybe we're not even inside my version of the dollhouse anymore."

"Where else would we be?" Sadie asked.

Nowhere . . . Alone . . . Lou shook the thought away and then waved the group toward the brighter passage.

But Cal nodded toward the darker one. "Let's try this way instead."

"Why *on earth* would we do that?" asked Sadie.

"In horror movies, the characters always seek the least frightening way out of dangerous situations. And most times, that choice ends up leading them directly into the belly of the beast . . . so to speak." Cal stepped around the corner into the shadow. "Let's change the game. If this house can move around and shift its form, there must be something controlling it that wants us to go into the light. We need to go the opposite way. *This* way."

Lou stood still, unwilling to step into the darker passage. She'd had enough darkness today. She took Sadie's elbow and pulled her close. "I don't like it," she whispered. "We're not in a horror movie, Cal."

"But scary stories follow patterns for a reason. People in these situations tend to behave in certain ways. I've watched enough of them to know. If this house understands what scares us, it'll keep playing with our expectations."

Sadie scowled. "What if it *expects* you to say this?"

"It expects us to fight," Cal reasoned. "Even with one another." He crossed his arms. For the first time since Lou had encountered him in the screening room, Cal looked annoyed. "So . . . it's doing a good job with that part of it."

"He's right." Sadie sighed. "We'll give you this one, Cal. But at the next fork in the path, Lou gets to choose. Okay?"

Cal nodded and then glanced at Lou.

Every bone in her body was begging her to stay in the light, but she turned and followed Cal as he headed toward the unlit passage.

CHAPTER 16

PUSHING THROUGH THE house's reflective surfaces, Connie brought Jason to the nursery room, where the boy and the girl were still butting heads.

Apparently, the girl, whose name was Nina, did not appreciate the boy's tone when he'd suggested they search for a way out. His name was Rufus. Nina wanted him to leave her alone. But Rufus claimed to have seen some spooky things while wandering the hallways and didn't think it was a good idea for either of them to head off by themselves. Nina didn't believe him.

"I don't know how many more times I can apologize to you," Rufus said to Nina. He was several inches taller than her, but he stooped to make himself seem smaller. "We need to get out of here. Now."

Jason glanced silently at Connie. How would he get their attention without frightening them like he had Louise?

Nina sighed and cupped her hands, calling out through them, "Mama! Auntie Kerani! Where are you?"

Jason waved his hands, trying to catch her attention through the reflection in the window, but she didn't notice.

Rufus plopped down into a wide, cushiony chair and threw his head into his hands. "You're just like all the girls at my school. Too pretty. You don't want to be seen with the 'big' kid."

"That's not true," Nina spat. "I mean, yes, I'm pretty, but not the other part."

"Riiight." He rolled his eyes. "Because you're just so unique."

Her skin reddened. "I'm like *me*. And *me alone*." After a moment, she took in his defeated posture, and then seemed to deflate a bit herself. "And you're wrong. I would never judge anyone for how they looked." She sauntered over to a chair near Rufus and perched on its wide armrest. "Tell me again about what scared you so badly."

"Why? So you can make fun of me?"

"I said I don't do that." She tugged at the hem of his black cowboy shirt. "Besides, I think your shirt is pretty cool. Though maybe not with shorts. There's an amazing vintage shop right around the corner from my house. I would suggest we head there right now, but somehow, I don't think we're in Florida anymore."

"Last I checked, I live in Kansas."

"And the last *I* checked, I'm not crazy."

"Either way, now isn't the time to think about shopping." He reached out and plucked at the shoulder of her dress. "Don't you worry about creepy-crawlies in those old secondhand stores?" he asked, holding up what looked like a thick white thread. "Bedbugs and stuff like that."

Nina flinched away from the object in his hand, and it fell to the floor. "My clothes do not have *bugs*! How disgusting."

"I'm sorry! It's just . . ." He bent down, peering at the threadlike thing at his feet.

Connie nudged Jason to stand behind the two again so they might see his reflection in the mirror. But Jason stood his ground, his eyes doubling in size. Connie hadn't noticed, like he had, that the "thread" Rufus plucked from Nina's dress was starting to squirm.

Rufus gasped. "*Geez* . . ." Nina tensed as Rufus stood and held up his hands. "Do *not* move."

"Why?" she yelped. "What is it?"

That's when Jason saw what was wrong: The thing that was squirming on the floor? There were more of them . . .

And they were crawling through Nina's hair. Glancing at Connie, he asked, "What do we do?"

"Catch Rufus's and Nina's attention," Connie answered quickly. "You need to get them both out of here. Now."

Rufus stood and quickly pulled the worms from Nina's head. She shrieked when she saw their wriggling bodies on the floor. She bent over and ran her hands through her hair, shaking it out, ruining her curls.

Jason stood behind them in the mirror and then waved his hands like a crossing guard at the end of a school day. But they were too busy freaking out to notice. Connie positioned herself on the other side and motioned to them from her reflection in the window.

"Did we get all of them?" Nina asked, her voice wobbly. She was twitchy, and rubbed at her arms.

Just then, Jason noticed another worm fall on her from above.

"*Oh, no,*" Connie whispered.

All of them looked up at the ceiling. A slim crack had split open the plaster just overhead. From inside, dozens of white, pin-like heads poked out, wiggling around as if feeling for a meal. Another of them dropped from the crack and plopped onto Nina's cheek. She screamed so hard that no sound came out, then she slapped at her face, leaving a red mark and a white smear.

Rufus shoved her out of the way as the crack widened like a smile. Hundreds of the little white worms spewed forth—*plop-plop-plop*—forming a mound on the floor below.

Jason's jaw dropped. He snapped it shut swiftly, as if one of the little creatures might jump up and hurtle through his lips.

Nina and Rufus raced across the room. Nina grabbed the knob of the nearest door, only to find herself staring into an empty closet. She slammed it shut and then pressed herself against it. Both she and Rufus stared in awe at the shower of worms that continued to rain down from the widening crack in the ceiling.

Connie called to Jason, "There's another door beside the mirror we came through. It leads to the hallway. There will be another mirror hanging out there. Point them to the stairs. I'll take care of this mess."

The mass of worms writhed, slowly forming a squirming column that stood nearly three feet high. The column began to slither across the floor, reaching out to Nina and Rufus, and Connie stepped in front of it, blocking its path.

Trembling, Jason sidled up beside Nina and Rufus. He had no clue how to shift their attention away from the horrific sight. "There's got to be a way out of here," Rufus said, scanning the nursery for another exit. Finally, he noticed the odd reflection in the mirror. "What the . . . ?"

Startled, Jason waved his hands over his head. Nina gasped when she saw him. But they didn't run or scream. Making sure to stay in their line of sight, Jason ran over to the door and gestured wildly at the exit. Moments later, the two were across the room, racing out into the hallway.

CHAPTER 17

LOU EXPECTED THE dark passage to lead them into a brighter space, but it only became gloomier. As the light darkened around her, so did Lou's thoughts.

She remembered her nightmares. In one, a girl followed a long pink string throughout the tangle of hallways until she'd reached a greenhouse filled with walking corpses. In another, the wallpaper reached out with poisonous tendrils, trying to grab at a few other kids. In another, a girl was trapped in a room, fire spreading around her and the air filling with black smoke.

There was growling nearby. Lou grabbed Sadie's shirt. When Sadie turned, her face was barely visible. "Did you hear that?" Sadie shook her head and kept walking. Cal didn't even pause. And Lou felt even more certain that following him in this direction had been a big mistake.

The sound was different now. A deep vibration, like when she'd stand underneath the elevated tracks in Walnut Creek as the commuter trains passed overhead. "Maybe we should go back," Lou whispered to the others, unable to control the waver in her voice. But Sadie and Cal moved even faster. So fast now that it seemed they were running. "Hey . . ." She tried to shout as quietly as she could. "Wait up. Don't leave me!"

The rumbling came again, resounding like a low chord on a piano. Lou realized that it *was* a low chord on a piano. A few more notes tinkled sadly around it, an improvised riff that was somehow familiar to Lou. The music seemed to be coming from inside the walls. Lou reached out blindly, but it was as if the hallway had expanded and her fingertips met only air.

Fury boiled in the back of her neck. She wished she could throttle Cal. The whole point of exploring the house was so she could locate another fireplace. How could she find any-thing if she couldn't even see her own hands in front of her?

Lou realized that she was suddenly alone. She couldn't hear Sadie or Cal up ahead of her anymore. Had they left her behind?

No, no, no . . . I can't take it anymore. Someone, please, help me . . .

Lou squeezed her eyes shut, praying that her racing heart would finally wake her from this nightmare.

As the music went on, a melody formed. The tune made her think of foggy days and the call of ships out on the bay. Lou focused on the music and took several deep breaths. In her mind, she heard Jason's voice saying *Everything is going to be all right*. She wasn't sure she believed it, but it helped somehow. As Lou listened, she thought she could pinpoint the direction the piano music was coming from. She allowed her instinct to pull her toward it.

She found herself standing before a closed door, the edges trimmed in a rectangle of amber light from the other side. Without knocking, Lou slowly swung the door inward. The room was long with high ceilings, decorated with green wallpaper. There were instruments and music stands and wooden chairs scattered all around. But in the center sat a glossy black grand piano. Its lid was propped open and whoever was playing was hidden around the other side. The dark notes swirled around the space, diving at Lou and then retreating, almost as if the music were alive. Lou held her breath as she circled the piano at a distance, bringing the player into view.

A boy, who was about Jason's height, sat on the piano bench with his eyes closed. His skin was pale, and his red hair was bunched in small, tight curls. His forehead was scrunched in concentration as his torso swayed and lurched, following his fingers up and down the keyboard.

Lou stepped on a weak floorboard, and it squeaked. The boy stopped playing and looked at her. His eyes went nuclear, and he stood, knocking the bench over. It hit the ground with a raucous bang.

Lou's jaw dropped as she realized who it was that she'd stumbled upon.

"Louise!" her cousin cried out. "What are you doing here?"

CHAPTER 18

"MARCUS!" LOU YELLED, running over and throwing her arms around him. The echo of her voice mixed with the lingering notes of her cousin's piano tune. "Everyone is looking for you! I can't believe . . ." She realized he was leaning away from her, and she stepped back. It had only been a few months since she'd seen him, but he looked so different. There were dark patches underneath his eyes, and his cheeks, which were normally so full and flushed, were sunken and pale. Even his bright red curls seemed dimmer. "Are you okay? Your parents are totally freaking out."

"Sounds like a normal day in the Geller household." He took her hands and squeezed.

"Your mom told us that you were missing. I flew with my mom to Cleveland. The police are involved and everything. We've got to get you home!"

Marcus glanced around the room. "This isn't good. This isn't good at all." He lowered his voice and whispered something gruffly to himself—something that sounded like, *Why her?*

"How do we get out of here, Marcus? The things that I've seen . . ."

Marcus shook his head. "Getting out of here might be harder than you think."

"I have a pretty good idea how hard it is. It's why I asked."

He gasped and then pulled Lou around the other side of the piano. "There are a couple kids in the doorway. Do you see them too?"

Lou realized that Sadie and Cal were watching her reunion with Marcus, and she let out a sigh of relief. "I thought you guys left me by myself."

Sadie raised an eyebrow. "We were right behind you the whole time."

Cal nodded. "We followed you here."

It didn't make sense. Lou had watched them run off ahead of her. Had something gotten into her head? Was the shadow creature from the movie screen trying to split them up? She didn't feel like hashing it out. They were all together now, and with Marcus here, Lou finally felt like they stood a chance against whatever dark powers were in control of the dollhouse. "Sadie . . . Cal . . . This is Marcus. My cousin."

"The one you were telling us about earlier?" Cal asked. Lou nodded.

Sadie stepped into the room. "That was you playing the piano?" Marcus nodded. "You're really good," she said. For the first time since they'd met, Lou noticed Sadie's eyes sparkle. Marcus shrugged. "I play too," she went on. "Well, I *used* to play, anyway. I'd love to start again." She looked around, taking in the number of instruments. "This room is amazing. What an inspiration."

"There aren't many places in this house where I feel safe," said Marcus. Lou thought it was a weird, almost non-answer.

"Me neither," said Cal, closing the door behind him.

"So if you were headed to a music school, how did you end up here?" Lou asked. "I found an email printout in your bedroom. It was an invitation from someone named L. Delphinium. It was addressed to your mom, but when I showed her, she didn't remember seeing it."

Marcus scoffed. "How could she not remember?" he said to himself with a shake of his head. "You're right, Louise. I came to Larkspur thinking it was a music school. Mom put me on the bus herself. When I got here, I found four other kids who arrived the same day I did. All of us had been invited for different reasons." He bent down and righted the piano bench. "Sit," he instructed, "and I'll explain what happened to us."

Marcus told the tale as he recalled it, though he admitted that some pieces were harder to reach than others. It had been a gathering of five: Poppy, Azumi, Dylan, Dash, and himself. Poppy had come to live with her great-aunt, Azumi for boarding school, Dylan and Dash to star in a scary movie, and Marcus for the music academy. None of these reasons were real. Something in the house had tricked them into showing up. "After we all stepped inside, the doors locked," Marcus said. "We found that the windows were unbreakable." And worse, a group of creepy children wearing animal masks pursued them relentlessly through the house. Marcus and the others ran from them, but they could not hide, no matter how hard they tried. Eventually, the five managed to find their way into the yard, but . . . "I can't remember much after that." Marcus paused. "I woke up at the edge of the woods sometime later. The other kids had left me. Alone. I scoured the property but I couldn't find the gate. It was like there was no way out. So I came back to the music room. The

instruments were still here. And playing calms me down."
He wiped at his damp eyes. "I thought . . . I thought I'd be
alone here forever." Glancing at Lou, he frowned. "You shouldn't
have come looking for me. Now you'll be stuck here too."

"But we're *not* stuck here," said Cal. "Lou has an idea
about how to escape. We've been searching for chimneys.
We'll climb up and out and then just scoot on home."

"The only thing is," said Lou, "the house keeps chang-
ing shape."

"Oh, yeah." Marcus nodded. "It tends to do that."

Sadie had wandered to the far end of the room and was
staring in wonder at the antique instruments. She gasped
and then called over to Marcus. "Was this here before?" She
pointed at an iron cage that was attached to the floor. It
appeared to have grown right through the green carpet, next
to a bookcase that was overflowing with sheet music. Inside,
propped against the thick bars, Lou noticed a stringed instrument that looked like a tiny guitar.

No. Not a guitar. A ukulele.

Marcus stared at it like it was a bomb. "I've been in this
room for what feels like forever, and this is the first time I've
noticed it." Sadie reached for the cage, but Marcus stopped
her. "Wouldn't do that if I were you."

"But . . . I think it's mine."

"You're welcome to play any of the instruments in here," he said. "They don't belong to anyone anymore."

Sadie shook her head. "No, I mean . . . I think it's *my* ukulele. The one my grandmother gave me." She glanced at Lou. "The one that broke during the competition. I was playing it just before I found myself in this crazy house." Cal, Lou, and Marcus came closer. "I *know* it's mine. It's got the same mark on the bottom of it. Look. There." The three crouched to glance at the underside of the ukulele. On its base, stamped into the glossy wood right where Sadie said it would be, was a strange symbol. It was a circle with several marks inside that might have been letters. "I figured that its previous owner marked it, but I've never learned what it meant."

Lou felt the blood drain from her head. She had to sit on the floor to keep from toppling over.

"What is it?" Marcus asked her. "What's wrong?"

She cleared her throat, which felt fuzzy all of a sudden. "You won't believe me."

Cal had a faraway look in his eyes. "I have a feeling that I will. We all will."

"My dollhouse has the same mark on its base," Lou exhaled.

Cal nodded. "So does the old camera I found in the woods by the Larkspur estate. There's a symbol on its back that makes it look like it could be siblings with the one on Sadie's ukulele."

Sadie stepped away from the cage. "What does it mean?"

"Isn't it obvious?" Cal answered. "Your ukulele. My camera. Her dollhouse. We each own an object that once lived at Larkspur House."

Silence filled the room for the first time since Lou had stepped inside.

Sadie clawed at the cage. "I have to get it out of there. I need to finish playing the song that I had stuck in my head earlier today. I need to know that I can figure it out. Lou, help me!" She grabbed the bars and shook them, but the cage wouldn't budge.

"Song?" Marcus asked, his expression turning grim. "What song?"

"It was something that just popped into my head." Sadie kept her eye on the cage, as if seeking a weak spot. "When I first heard the tune, it was like there was music playing in another room. Coming to me through the walls."

Marcus stepped between Sadie and the cage. "*In another room?*" he echoed.

"What's wrong, Marcus?" Lou asked, taking his hand and tugging him aside. "You're getting upset. Why?"

"I can hum it for you." Sadie had a wild look in her eyes, as if she couldn't stand to be apart from the ukulele for one second more.

"Don't!" Marcus cried out.

But Sadie didn't listen. She hummed softly, a gentle melody that struck Lou in her stomach like a fist.

"Stop," Marcus said. "Please. You don't know what you're doing. It hates that tune. You'll bring it straight to us!"

"*It?*" The word made Lou feel very small and useless. "What is *it*?" she asked, knowing exactly what her cousin had meant.

Sadie went on humming, as if she hadn't heard a word of Marcus's warning.

Cal tugged on the strap of her overalls. "Maybe you should listen to him," he whispered. Sadie only made her voice louder.

Marcus was frantic now. "The creature! The monster that . . . You have no idea what I've seen." He took her chin and looked into her eyes. "Stop, Sadie, please. I'm begging you."

She looked at him as if he'd suddenly materialized before her. "I'm sorry," she whispered. "I didn't—"

But it was too late.

The room shook, and a fissure raced up the wall from floor to ceiling, splitting the green wallpaper and knocking the bookcase forward.

CHAPTER 19

THE GROUP SCATTERED, shocked into silence. Leaves of sheet music spilled out across the floor, the papers lifting and swirling, propelled by the shaking.

Marcus faced the door of the music room and then waved for the others to follow him. "Go now! Quickly!"

Cal and Lou raced across the room, but Sadie stood still, staring at the cage. As Marcus ran back to get her, the crack widened farther. Smaller ruptures split off from the main fissure, and pieces of plaster pushed out from the edge and fell to the floor. Growls and groans spewed forth from inside. Something was trying to shove its way through.

Marcus grabbed at Sadie's arm, but she wiggled away. "*I need it*," she said, then leapt for the cage.

"Sadie, get back!" Lou yelled.

But Sadie did the opposite. She shoved her hands through the iron bars and seized the ukulele. She turned it around like a puzzle piece that might fit through one of the spaces.

The room shuddered, and a deafening shriek burst out from behind the wall. The crack spread from the wall to the floor boards, wrenching them apart beneath the cage. Sadie kicked at the wood until a wide gap appeared beneath the metal bars, even as a gust of air lifted her braids from her shoulders.

Lou was certain that the thing inside the wall was about to burst into the room and devour everyone. She pressed herself against the door, barely able to watch and too frightened to pull her friend to safety. "Sadie!"

Sadie reached through the gap and took the ukulele. She stared at the instrument as if she couldn't believe what she'd just done. Marcus rushed over and grabbed her elbow, then towed her toward the door.

A massive wallop jolted the wall from the other side. The crack split open into a wider crevice, wide enough for Lou to make out something large and black moving around just inside it. When Marcus and Sadie reached the exit, Lou threw the door open, and they all tumbled into the hallway. A deafening cry trumpeted out from behind them—a mix of rage and panic.

Lou slammed the door shut and took off, running down the hallway after Marcus and the others.

Jason and Connie had stepped through the mirror into the dining room—gesturing for Rufus and Nina to follow from another mirror down the hall—when a chorus of screams erupted out through the glass portal.

One of the voices sounded like Lou.

Jason's heart felt like it stopped. "What's happening now?" he asked Connie. Had the worms in the nursery flooded the rest of the house? Or was it some new horror? She shook her head in confusion, then vanished. Reappearing a moment later, she said, "The group is right around the corner from here. There's no sign of the creature. Something else must have scared them."

Jason nearly went limp with relief.

Rufus waved to Jason's reflection. "Which way?" he asked. Nina looked at herself in the mirror and tried to quickly fix her hair.

Connie pointed to an open doorway.

"This is where you were leading us?" Nina asked. "There are others here? They're . . . *friendly*?"

Connie and Jason nodded emphatically.

Nina and Rufus glanced at each other before stepping through.

"Who are you?"

The voice had come from behind Lou. She turned, and nearly stumbled backward. Two kids were standing in the doorway to the kitchen, blocking the way out. The girl crossed her arms, trying to look tough, and the boy hunched his shoulders as if he were trying to disappear.

"Well?" asked the girl in the doorway. Her messy black hair fell in frizzy ringlets to her shoulders. Even though she looked intimidating, Lou figured that she didn't look *scary*, which was a good thing.

"I'm Lou Benjamin," said Lou. She introduced the others quickly, not knowing what else to say other than, "And who are you?"

"I'm Nina Patel."

"Rufus Mendoza," the boy answered.

For a few seconds, everyone just stared at one another, waiting for someone else to make a move, and Lou looked around the huge kitchen where they'd all ended up.

A dim bulb over the iron stove cast a faint light across the shadowed space. Behind her was a long counter whose surface looked like a giant chopping block. Large cabinets lined the walls and an immense steel refrigerator hulked in the far corner.

"You guys know the way out?" Rufus asked.

"We're working on it," said Cal.

Nina turned to Rufus and groaned. "I thought the kids in the mirror were going to help us leave this place."

Rufus nodded at the others. "Maybe we're all just supposed to work together?"

"Kids in the *mirror*?" Lou repeated. It made her think of her brother's reflection in the window and the movie screen, how he'd tried to frighten her.

Nina tilted her head as she gave Lou a funny glance. "You kind of look like the boy."

"What boy?"

"In the mirror! You have the same eyes. And there was a girl wearing an old-fashioned black dress with a white apron over it."

Rufus went on. "The boy and the girl appeared in the mirror in the nursery upstairs. For some reason, we couldn't hear them." Lou stiffened. This sounded too familiar. "They showed us the way out of the room, away from the worms." *Worms?* Lou wondered, but Rufus left her no time to ask. "We went where they pointed, only to find *another* mirror with them in it, pointing us in a new direction. Mirror after mirror. Hallway after hallway. Finally, we found ourselves down here, in that huge dining room across the way." Rufus wiped at his forehead. "I've never seen such a big house. Have you?"

Jason had been helping them? Lou didn't want to believe it. Was the house playing more tricks on her, trying to make her think that Jason was actually here? Did it want her to trust him, to give her hope, only so it could snatch it away again? To make her feel even *more* abandoned? She stepped back from the two new kids.

"You look like you don't believe us," Nina said. "Why not?"

Lou sighed. After a moment, she explained what she and Sadie and Cal and Marcus had just been through.

Marcus is here in the house? Jason blinked, staring through the doorway to the kitchen, wondering if the sight of his cousin was another trick.

When Jason and Connie had combed through the dollhouse from the outside, they hadn't noticed anyone else but the five kids and the shadow thing creeping through the hallways. What a relief to see him! If Jason wasn't able to stand beside Lou and protect her, at least their cousin was.

Jason couldn't see much of the exchange from his spot in the dining room, but he heard all of it.

"Why did the house choose us?" asked Nina.

"Maybe it has something to do with this." Sadie showed them the symbol on the ukulele she'd found in the music room. "The symbol proves that the ukulele is the same one that my grandmother gave to me."

"*Symbol?*" Connie whispered to herself, startling Jason.

"Does that mean something to you?" he asked. Connie glanced worriedly at him, but kept listening.

"There was the same symbol on some objects that belonged to us too," said Cal. "My antique camera back home. And Lou's dollhouse—the one that resembles the mansion we're standing in right now."

"I bet they were all marked by the same person," said Lou.

"Or people," said Sadie.

Nina extended her hand toward Sadie's ukulele. "Can I see that?" She turned it over and examined the bottom of it closely, running a finger over the carved mark. Her breath hitched, and she shuddered. "I have a piece of clothing that I got at the vintage shop near my house. A black cloak. Beautiful chiffon. Very expensive, but I got it for a steal! None of the other girls at my school had any clue how special it was." She rolled her eyes. "But . . . the thing is . . . there's a white tag on the inside of the cloak's collar." She pointed at

Sadie's ukulele. "This same symbol is sewn right in the middle of my cloak's tag." She passed the instrument back to Sadie.

Rufus spoke up too. "A while back, when my mom and me were visiting family in Louisiana, I found a sketchbook in a table at our motel. Half of the sketchbook was already filled with drawings of a creepy-looking dude. I've been using the blank half of the book to draw my own comic sketches."

"Let me guess," said Marcus. "There's a symbol in your sketchbook?"

Rufus nodded, his eyes wide with amazement and fear.

As the group continued to converse, Jason noticed Marcus move into view through the sliver of the kitchen doorway. It seemed as though Marcus was looking straight at him. *He can see me!* Jason thought. Maybe he could signal to Marcus, to pass Lou a message from him. *I'm here. Don't be scared.* He was about to raise his hand when Marcus furrowed his brow and turned away. A moment later, the doorway from the dining room to the hall and the kitchen disappeared.

In its place was a wall.

CHAPTER 20

"I THINK THAT the boy in the mirror really might be your brother," Rufus said to Lou.

Cal nodded. "It would be a great twist."

"Twist?" asked Nina.

Sadie rolled her eyes. "Cal thinks that everything happening here is part of some horror movie."

Cal scowled. "At least I don't feel the need to hug a ukulele."

Sadie's expression went flat, and she loosened her grip on the instrument.

Nina chuckled. "Part of a horror movie? *That's* weird."

"I can show you the mirror where we last saw him," Rufus went on. "He's probably still there. He might even be able to show us the way out of here. Come on. It was back this way through the—" But the kitchen door was gone. Now there was only a flat white wall, decorated by shadows cast from the light over the stove.

Nina covered her mouth.

"The house changes shape," said Marcus with a lump in his throat. "Haven't you noticed?"

Nina closed her eyes. "I didn't want to believe it." Rufus tried to pat her shoulder, but she wriggled away from him. "Don't touch me!"

"I'm sorry!"

"You guys: Don't fight," Lou pleaded. "We need to stick together. Now more than ever." She looked to Marcus. "Is there another way out of the kitchen?"

"You mean other than the windows?" He pointed to the dark glass that was far from their reach.

"Glass here doesn't break," Sadie said.

"So we're just stuck?" Cal asked. "In scary movies, moments like this usually mean the characters are supposed to figure something out."

"Like what?" asked Nina, sticking out her chin. "Who's going to *die* next?"

Cal's eyebrows flicked up in surprise. Everyone else looked at Nina like she'd just kicked a kitten. She lowered her gaze to the floor and turned around, embarrassed. Cal went on, "I was gonna say maybe we should think about other ways out. There has to be something. If the house keeps us locked in here, then the story dies."

"Unless us dying in this room *is* the story," said Nina.

"Stop talking about dying, please," Marcus whispered. "It's . . . *disturbing*."

Sadie spun, as if she'd heard footsteps creeping up behind her. "What was that?" There was nothing there.

"That question is getting old," said Cal.

"I'm sorry," Sadie said. "But I know I heard something. It sounded like it came from . . . inside the refrigerator."

Everyone looked to the refrigerator in the corner of the room, but it was silent. *The fridge back home hums constantly,* Lou thought, *so what's wrong with this one?*

After several seconds, Sadie piped up again. "I swear it was—" The chrome handle rattled slightly.

Nina let out an earsplitting shriek. The group jumped in surprise and then scrambled collectively toward the white wall where the doorway had stood.

CHAPTER 21

NINA CLAWED AT the wall as if she might dig her way to freedom. She broke a couple of fingernails, and soon she'd streaked the white surface with red.

"Stop it," said Lou softly, grabbing at Nina's hands and pulling them down by Nina's side. "You'll only hurt yourself more."

Nina slumped to the floor, weeping, holding her hands to her face. "Mama . . . Auntie Kerani . . . Please find me," she mumbled.

The refrigerator door rattled again. This time, a little harder. The group turned from Nina and waited for it to happen again.

Lou bent down and rubbed at Nina's shoulder, surprised that the jumpy girl wasn't complaining. In fact, Nina turned her cheek and wiped her tears on Lou's arm. The wetness was kind of gross, but Lou didn't mind. She figured that they'd all discovered their own method of finding comfort. Sadie hugged her ukulele tighter. Cal needed to relate his experience as part of a story. Marcus had told them that playing the piano in the music room had been his balm. She wasn't sure about Rufus yet, and Nina seemed to appreciate kindness from the women in her life—her mom and aunt, and now Lou. She thought about her brother. If Jason really was trapped somewhere in this house—as Rufus and Nina believed—how was he getting through it without breaking into pieces? Lou half hoped that he was here with her in some form; but the other half of her wished he were far from here, dreaming clueless dreams.

Something slammed at the fridge door from inside, and it rocked in place for several seconds. Nina screamed again, pressing the heels of her palms into her eyes. Sadie groaned, squeezing the ukulele so tightly the strings squeaked.

"We have to remain calm," said Lou.

"How?" asked Rufus, trembling.

"I know how," Cal answered, stepping away from the group. "We open the refrigerator door."

Sadie stomped on the floor and glared at him. "That sounds like a bad, *bad* idea, Cal."

Cal shrugged. "Not at all. If we don't want our story to end in this room, our only option is to see what's inside."

"I'm with Sadie." Nina stood, her fists clenched. "Don't. You. Dare."

"The house wants us scared," Cal said. "So waiting to see what happens here will only hurt us in the long run. If we open the door, we learn what's inside. It could be terrifying, but it could also be nothing at all. Not *knowing* can be more frightening than having the scariest answer."

Nina glared at him. "You can't be serious."

Sadie shook her head and then pointed at Cal, her finger trembling. "If we were standing at the edge of a cliff, we'd feel scared about falling and hitting the rocks below. But we wouldn't step off the ledge just to stop worrying about it."

"You're missing my point," said Cal. "This isn't about leaping. It's about learning the truth."

"And you're missing *my* point," said Sadie. "Sometimes, when we learn the truth, we wish we still knew only the lie. By not knowing, *hope* can live on."

"Yeah, well, by that logic, we might as well just stand here and close our eyes, hoping that we'll magically wake up at home." He turned his back on her and walked toward the refrigerator.

Everyone called out for him to stop, but Sadie was the only one who took off after him. Placing her ukulele on the floor, she grabbed his elbow and pulled him backward. Lou cried out, "Sadie, no!"

"Get off me," Cal grumbled. He yanked himself away and then dashed closer to the refrigerator.

It thumped and shook again.

"Please, Cal! Don't!" Sadie called.

Cal smirked and reached for the door. "You'll see."

To everyone's shock, the handle moved by itself, and the door squeaked slowly open.

CHAPTER 22

LOU WATCHED, STUNNED, as Cal peered into the refrigerator. She was waiting for the door to burst wide, smacking him in the chest and launching him backward into Sadie.

But nothing happened.

Cal gagged and then covered his mouth and nose with his hand. "Holy crud, it stinks."

Sadie stepped away, and Cal dragged the door open fully. From where she stood with the others, Lou could only make out darkness inside.

Cal leaned forward and then shook his head in amazement. "You guys have to check this out," he said, rubbing at his throat, trying to not gag again.

"Is it empty?" asked Rufus.

"Sort of. But . . . you need to see for yourselves to understand."

"Sadie?" Lou called out.

Sadie turned toward her, her eyes wide and red, nodding slightly.

Nina, Rufus, Marcus, and Lou made their away around the butcher-block island.

As she came closer to the open door, Lou understood why Cal looked like he wanted to throw up. The smell was worse than at her condo's Dumpster on the hottest summer day. Its surfaces were green with mold and dripping with black slime, and Lou wondered if she'd ever have an appetite again.

But it wasn't the smell or the slime that had captured Cal's and Sadie's attention. Where the rear wall should have been, there was nothing. The space just went on and on like a garbage chute sloping downward into the earth. At the far end, there was a pinpoint of light.

"A way out," said Cal. Taking a deep breath, he stepped into the refrigerator and then disappeared into the darkness.

Nina grabbed Lou and squeezed her like a rag doll. "I can't do this!"

"We have to," said Rufus. Covering his mouth with his hand, he followed Cal. Sadie pressed her lips shut in silent

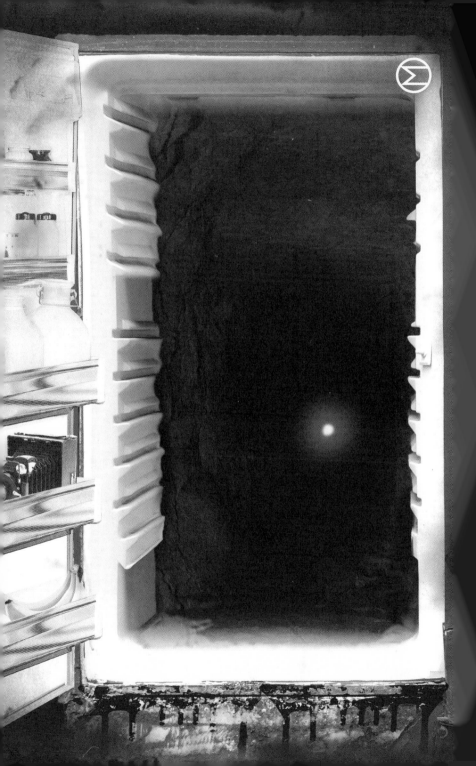

anger as she too stepped inside, clinging to her ukulele. She didn't even look back.

"I'll stay here," said Nina. "You guys can send for help."

Marcus shook his head. "This place doesn't work that way."

Lou listened as the others slipped and slid down the slope. No one was screaming or whimpering or making any noise at all. Was this a good sign, or bad? "Come on," she said to Nina. "Marcus will go ahead of you. And I'll go behind. You'll be safe between us."

"But what *is* that stuff?" Nina asked, gesturing to the black rot that was coating the walls.

"Don't think about it," said Marcus, taking her hand. To Lou's surprise, Nina stepped through the doorway.

Lou followed. She tried to not touch the walls, but the floor was so slippery, she had to reach to remain upright. She pressed her hands into the cold slime until her palms met a solid surface several inches underneath. She kept the back of her throat closed and forced herself to think of the wildflowers that grew on Mount Diablo, of her mother's sweet perfume that she wore to temple, of the crisp scent of the balsa wood she'd used to make dollhouse furniture.

The space inside the refrigerator was slim—only about two and a half feet wide and maybe four feet tall. The slope descended much more steeply than Lou had anticipated. Nina walked slowly before her, sliding and skidding to a stop with nearly every step. Marcus called out to them from up ahead. "You two okay back there?"

"So far so good," said Lou. But Nina only murmured, "Mmmm." *Was that a yes or no?* Lou wondered. They'd made it a few yards and had about a dozen to go.

Wham!

The tunnel trembled.

Glancing over her shoulder, Lou discovered the refrigerator door had slammed shut. The sound of squealing metal and crunching ceramic blasted from the darkness. It took a moment for Lou to understand what she was seeing: the tunnel was collapsing behind them, squeezing in on itself, as if someone were clenching it like a tube of toothpaste.

Ahead, Nina was frozen with terror. She pushed at the sides of the tunnel as if trying to keep herself in place. "Go forward!" Lou yelled. "Hurry!"

But Nina only answered with "No, no, no, no, no . . ."

Crunch!

The top of the tunnel dipped several inches. Lou dropped to a crouch.

Crunch!

She looked back again. It was dark, but Lou could tell that the collapse was coming closer—too close for comfort. "You have to move, Nina, or we are both going to be crushed."

Nina released a tight-lipped wail, but she didn't budge.

Crunch!

Now Lou could feel pressure by her toes. There was no room to adjust her feet. If the tunnel flattened any farther forward . . .

Lou reached out and pushed at Nina's back. She shrieked as Lou shoved her and then lost her footing. Nina fell face-first into the sludge on the tunnel floor. "UGH!" she cried. "My clothes!"

There was enough room now for Lou to crawl over her and down the chute by herself, but there was no way Lou could leave Nina behind.

Marcus called out to them from the bottom of the slope. "What's taking you two so long?"

Lou didn't want to risk *him* crawling back inside to get them, so she called out, "Coming!" She grabbed the bottom of Nina's feet and pushed with all her strength. Crying, Nina slid a few inches. Lou crept forward and then shoved at her again. This time when Nina slid, she didn't stop. The sludge was too slick. Nina vanished down the slope, screaming as if she were careening to the bottom of a waterslide.

Crunch!

Lou scrabbled through the muck. She needed to push herself forward, but the walls were too slippery. She closed her eyes, spread her fingers out, and pressed down. Swiping her arms downward, Lou propelled herself forward like a bullet. The light at the end of the passage grew brighter and wider, and then Lou was tumbling across a stone floor into a new space.

She was lying on her back, bruised and battered and struggling for breath, when another *crunch* echoed out from inside the tunnel and a massive wave of the black sludge poured from the opening in the wall and spread in a giant puddle all around her.

The stench was dizzying. More so than before. Lou was too shaken to move.

Moments later, after wiping her face clean, Lou opened her eyes to find Marcus, Cal, and Sadie leaning over her, holding out their hands to help her up.

But Nina was off by herself, crouched against a wall, slathered in gunk and wearing an expression of shock.

CHAPTER 23

AFTER LOU HAD gotten to her feet, Nina called out to the group. "Is everybody happy? We're not in the kitchen anymore, but is this place any better?" She ran both hands through her long hair, squeezing the foul liquid from it. "At least before I didn't smell like my little brother's diaper bin!"

"This is awful," said Rufus, shuddering.

Cal piped up. "But we're not worrying about what might be hiding in the fridge anymore. So that's good. Right?"

"If you say so," answered Sadie. She turned her ukulele over and drained the goop that had collected inside it.

"It *is* good," said Marcus. "We've got to stay calm. And quiet. We don't want the house to know where we are."

"Where *are* we?" asked Rufus.

She looked around, but the compact room was lit only by a pale reflected glow that came in through what looked like a hole in the ceiling. The walls were constructed of ancient stone. "I don't recognize this place," she said. "Marcus?" Her cousin shook his head.

Sadie approached a crate that sat in the middle of the floor. It was made of metal wires and looked large enough to house a Rottweiler. "It's a kennel," she whispered. She gestured to the shadows, where many more cages were stacked along the walls.

As Lou scanned the room, she thought she heard the distant sound of barking. And when she approached one of the crates, for a moment, she thought she saw a large black dog lunging toward her.

Scrambling back, she tripped over her feet and fell into the sludge again. From the ground, she saw that the crate was definitely empty.

She also noticed a pile of long, thick bones beside her. Femurs. Antlers. Ribs. The pale light from overhead allowed Lou to see gnaw marks left on them by sharp teeth. If this place had once lodged the dogs of Larkspur House, these bones might have been their last treats. Lou scrambled away. "I think it would be best if we got out of here as soon as possible," she said.

"There are no doors," said Marcus. "I already checked."

Cal pointed up. "That's got to lead somewhere."

"The hole in the ceiling?" Nina asked. "How would we reach it?"

"I wish Lou's brother and that other girl were still here with us," said Rufus. "I wish we had a mirror. They'd know where to send us."

"I wish the same thing," Lou said.

Cal pulled one of the crates directly underneath the hole. Climbing on top of the crate, he stretched out his arms; the gap between him and the ceiling was now only several feet. "Help me stack some more of these. We'll use the crates like blocks."

"And then what?" asked Nina. "Climb blindly into another tunnel? So we can end up in another creepy room with no doors?"

"Name another option," said Cal. "Just one."

Rufus shrugged. "I'm not sure I'd even be able to fit through this one, Cal."

"And how can I climb while carrying this thing?" Sadie asked, raising the ukulele.

"You could always just drop it," Cal suggested. Sadie squinted at him. "We're not staying down here. And there's no other way out." Not waiting for an answer, he dragged another two crates over to the first. "A little help?" Rufus reluctantly lifted one on top of the other. Sliding the three crates together, they became giant steps leading up to the shaft. Cal went to the top and craned his neck, peeking into the passage. "There's a hatch in the side only a few feet farther up. If we can make it—"

"Who's there?" Rufus interrupted. He glanced around, then turned to the others, shaking. "Did anyone else hear *people* calling out my name?"

"People?" asked Lou. "What people?"

"They . . . they sounded like the boys from my school," he whispered. "The bullies."

Barking filled the room.

Lou cringed. Nearby, the shadow-dog she'd seen lunge at her reappeared inside its crate. Its black body was transparent, but its teeth were as white as stars. They bit out at the wires, rattling them.

Slowly, dogs faded into the crates around the room— cages jammed with furious shadows whose gleaming canines chomped and dripped with shimmering saliva.

Thankfully, the doors were all still shut.

"Come on," Lou shouted. "Everyone move."

She grabbed Nina's hand and made sure she went first this time. Nina didn't argue as Cal boosted her up. Lou watched her feet disappear into the chute. The rest of them climbed onto the makeshift steps, the crates wobbling under their weight.

Sadie went up next. She used one hand to reach up into the shaft while the other pressed against her side, trapping the ukulele beneath it.

All at once, the cage doors around the room swung open. Silhouettes of a dozen black dogs leapt out. Lou groaned and hugged herself while Rufus kicked out at the leaping shadows. "Get away from me!" he shrieked. "Leave me alone!"

Cal and Marcus focused on lifting Sadie in to the ceiling.

One of the phantom dogs latched on to Rufus's sneaker. Rufus howled as the shadow shook at his foot. The stacked crates wobbled even harder. As Rufus yanked his foot away, he rolled off the crate and hit the floor with a solid *whump*!

The room hushed as all the dogs zeroed in on him.

"No, no, no . . . ," he groaned.

Voices whispered about the room, echoing off the stone walls. "*Ruuufuuuussss . . . We've found you . . . Can't sneak away now, can you?*"

"Stop it," Rufus choked out. "I-I never did anything to you."

Lou called to him from atop the crate. "Don't listen, Rufus. It's only the house, trying to scare you. They can't actually hurt you!"

"Ohhhh," said the voices, rising in unison, becoming a growl, and then several sharp barks. "Yes! We! Can!" The shadow-dogs rushed him, and Rufus scrambled back, through the slime, and pressed himself against the wall. One of the shadows snagged Rufus's calf. Another bit at his arm. He yelped, punching out at the shadows.

"No!" Lou shouted, leaping down. *Bad dogs!*" She picked up one of the bones from the floor and threw it. It passed right through the shadow-dogs and smacked against the stone wall beside Rufus. And for a moment, the creatures paused their attack, fixating briefly on the bone.

Rufus crawled toward Lou. She helped him to his feet as the shadow-dogs focused on them both and then charged.

Lou and Rufus swerved around the other side of the crates, jostling them. Cal and Marcus lost their grip on Sadie and she slipped down.

The ukulele caught on the bottom edge of the chute and slipped out from under Sadie's arm. Lou tried to grab it but she was too late.

It hit the ground below and splintered.

Inside the tunnel, Sadie screamed as if she had broken too, and then she dropped down onto the top crate with the others. She fell to her knees and reached out to the ukulele below.

"What are you guys doing down there?" came Nina's voice from the chute.

The shadow-dogs approached, sniffing and growling at the remains of the instrument. One of them even snapped at the broken wood and tangle of string, catching it in its jaws and whipping it back and forth.

Rufus and Lou scrambled up onto the crates and away from the gleaming teeth. Then, looking up at the chute, Rufus gasped. "Sadie, what's happening to you?"

Sadie was becoming translucent. Lou stared in horror. She could see right through her.

"I don't know," Sadie said, her eyes focusing on something directly in front of her—something that was invisible to the others. "I can see my bedroom! I think . . . I think I'm going home."

Before anyone could answer, she was gone.

CHAPTER 24

SUDDEN TREMORS ROCKED the house, stronger than any of the quakes that had occurred earlier.

The shadow-dogs howled at the sounds of cracking stone and breaking foundations. Marcus took Lou's arm and nudged her into place beneath the hole in the ceiling. "I'm not letting you go last this time," he said. The image of a dissolving Sadie flashed through her mind, and she nearly screamed as Marcus and Cal lifted her up. She palmed at the side of the chute, pressing her elbows outward to keep from spilling back down again. She felt the boys push at her legs and feet until she was fully inside the chute.

Sadie's words—*going home*—echoed through Lou's mind. She blinked them away as something brushed against her face from above.

Looking up, she saw Nina's filthy hand extended through a square hatch in the side of the shaft. Lou grabbed hold of it as another great shudder rattled the house and almost sent her tumbling back down into the kennel. Moments later, Nina managed to pull her up. Lou fell onto another tile floor.

The house let out a cry of pain. Dust rained down from above. "This place is about to collapse," said Lou, remembering the terror of the earthquakes back in California.

"Then help me!" Nina said, shoving herself back into the wall's hatch. As the walls groaned and cracks rent the ceiling, the girls helped pull Cal and Marcus up from the basement. Then all of them crowded at the hatch, straining to drag Rufus into the room. His slick clothes allowed him to slide through the small hole with barely a grunt.

"Where's Sadie?" asked Nina.

Before anyone could answer, a roaring explosion sounded from inside the hatch and smoke spewed out.

"Sadie's gone," said Marcus, bolting for the door several yards away.

Nina trembled. "She's dead?"

"No," said Lou. "She's *gone*. But we'll be dead if we stand here any longer." And with that, they trailed Marcus out into a new hallway.

Jason and Connie were standing outside the dollhouse in the dim light of the ghostly path.

They watched as a large wing on the right side of the house turned gray and brittle—like a dead branch on a living tree—and then crumbled to pieces. The roof caved in, then the walls tumbled down. Silently. Like ashes falling.

When it was done, the rest of the dollhouse stood as solidly as before. The lights in the windows flickered once.

Jason closed his eyes and breathed rapidly through his nose.

Connie took his hand, but her cold fingers were no comfort.

She's still alive. She has to be alive. She's the reason I'm here.

A moment later, voices echoed out of the dollhouse, not far from the destruction. Lou spoke clearly above the others, and Jason fell to his knees, heaving with relieved sobs. Connie knelt beside him. Together, they listened and learned what had caused the collapse.

"I think it happened when Sadie dropped her ukulele," said Lou, "and it smashed on the basement floor."

"Exactly," said Cal. "That's when she disappeared."

"She said she saw her bedroom," Rufus added. "Where she was heading. *Home*."

"I have an idea," said Connie. "Your sister will be okay for now. Come with me." She squeezed Jason's hand tightly and closed her eyes.

A moment later, he found himself in a room that looked like an art studio. Several easels stood in various corners, blank canvases propped upon them. Jars of dark water sat on window ledges and tables. The jars were jammed with brushes of all kinds and sizes. A freestanding mirror stood beside one of the easels, and a stool sat in front of it. On the walls, frames hung, containing paintings of mountains and rivers and sunsets. Other frames contained portraits of important-looking people. One man's face appeared again and again, and in each painting, he appeared to be older, as if captured at different points along his lifeline. When he was young, his eyes were stony and cold, but in the paintings of his elderly years, they appeared to be tinged with wildness.

"My father worked in here," said Connie. Steering clear of these portraits, she wandered to a small bookshelf along one wall. "He was a painter, and he achieved great success at a very young age. But he had help," she added. She scanned the shelves as if looking for a particular book. "Father belonged to a secretive men's club in New York City." She faced Jason, a serious look on her face. "These were bad men. They believed in monsters and acted as their guardians."

"Monsters?" Jason repeated, unsure he'd heard her correctly.

She nodded. "It was these men who told my father which parcel of land to buy in Greencliffe and where exactly to build the house. They knew of the creature who haunted those grounds, of the rewards it would give in return for a little . . . *sacrifice*. They taught Father how to make a pact. They taught him . . . a lot of things." Connie clenched her jaw and stared into the distance for a few seconds, collecting her emotions. Jason imagined that if her father were to appear—here and now—she'd have some not very nice words to say to him. Turning back to the bookshelves, her eyes grew bright. "Ah . . . here it is!" She pointed to the spine of one particular book. Burned into its leather was a symbol—a circle with lines inside that looked like overlapping letters . . . or maybe even a skull.

Jason was confused. "Is this like the markings that my sister and the other kids were talking about earlier? The ones they noticed on their objects?"

Connie nodded. "The members of my father's secret club would send him notes and drawings. Sometimes they'd send him handwritten books. This ledger is one of them."

Jason raised an eyebrow. "It came from your dad's secret society?"

"*Society*," Connie echoed, as if tasting the word. "Yes, *that's* what they'd called it. The Shadow Society."

"So what does it say?" Jason asked. He reached out to grab the book from the shelf, but his hand seemed to bounce off it. There was a barrier between them and the objects inside the house. It must be the reason Connie used the mirrors to travel from room to room. His skin grew cold at the thought. "There's no way to look inside it?" he asked hopelessly.

Connie raised an eyebrow and faced the mirror a few steps away. "I've discovered a method. Stand back."

Jason looked into the mirror. He gasped when swirls of black smoke appeared at the edges. There wasn't any smoke in the room—none that he could see—but it was in the reflection, growing thicker and thicker, until the smoke was so dense and dark, it almost entirely obscured Connie's image. He didn't know if he should say something. It was possible that Connie was making this happen, but he didn't think she was. The smoke reminded him of the creature.

Was she calling to the thing? Trying to bring it here? Or maybe she was fighting it?

Connie began to shake. Her face grew paler and looked damp, clammy, as if she were becoming ill. The glass was black now; the smoke had choked out all parts of the reflection. She bent forward slightly, looking like she might vomit.

"Connie," he whispered. He was about to touch her arm when she jolted backward, straightening upright, drawing her mouth up into a painful grimace. Then she opened her eyes and turned to look at him, slumping and stumbling away from the blackened mirror. "What happened?"

Connie fought to catch her breath. "It was trying to stop me," she said, her voice ragged.

"Stop you from doing what?"

"From retrieving the book." She reached into the deep pocket at the front of her white pinafore apron, but then her face went blank. She removed her hand to find that it was empty. She patted at her apron.

Whatever she'd been trying to do hadn't worked.

A soft voice spoke from near the bookshelf. "Were you trying to grab this?" They jolted and spun.

Marcus stood only a few feet away, watching them, holding a book.

CHAPTER 25

"MARCUS!" JASON CRIED out. "You can see us?"

"Of course I can see you," Marcus answered. "And you can see me!"

Warmth rushed into Jason's cheeks. "I'm so happy that you're all right."

Marcus smiled sadly. "But am I?"

"You've got to tell Lou that I'm here. That me and Connie will help her get out. But we need to flip through that book you're holding, to see if there are any other clues about how to do it."

"Don't worry," Marcus answered. "You keep yourselves safe. *I'm* going to help them."

"But Marcus—" Before Jason could finish, his cousin rushed out of the room and closed the door, taking the book with him. Shocked, Jason and Connie stood in the center of the room. "What just happened?"

Connie swallowed. "Your cousin said he's going to help them."

"I heard him. But . . . he took our book! Why would he do that?"

"He didn't think we needed it?" Connie closed her eyes and sighed.

"That's weird, right?" asked Jason. "It's just . . . Who exactly did he mean? *Who* is Marcus going to help?"

"I don't think we can leave it all up to him, no matter what he said. It's hard to trust anyone in this house. We must learn the truth ourselves."

Something clicked inside Jason's mind. "Part of the house fell apart after Sadie smashed her ukulele. Then she said she saw her bedroom. She thought she was going home. And then she disappeared." Connie straightened her spine and nodded. "Maybe . . . Maybe the other marked objects are located in the dollhouse too. If the group smashes them like Sadie's ukulele, maybe the house will release them too!"

Connie held her hands in front of her apron and gave him a satisfied smile. "I like how you think, Jason Benjamin. If we can locate the rest of the objects, we can point the kids in the right direction."

Jason nodded. "So . . . we look through the dollhouse. And when we find what we're looking for, we find a way to contact the group again. We tell them where to go and what to do."

"It'll be harder this time," said Connie.

"Harder? Why?"

She nodded at the black mirror across the room. "It knows we're here. It knows my tricks. If we need a reflection to communicate with them, the house will do everything it can to make that impossible."

"So . . . no more mirror portals?"

"We've got to be clever." Glancing around the room, she looked worried that even the air might be listening to them. "Follow me." She took Jason's hand and brought him outside again.

All this growing and shrinking was making him dizzy.

Connie unlatched the clasp at the dollhouse's roofline and swung it open. The group of kids were on the first level of the house, heading down a hallway that led to a cavernous room Jason hadn't seen before. But they were frozen, like the last time he'd opened the dollhouse. And Marcus was with them again, his curly red hair made of yarn and sprouting out of a cotton-sack head.

"Okay," said Connie. "The ukulele's cage was inside the music room. If the other objects follow that logic, we should be looking in places where the object typically belongs."

"Right," said Jason. "We've got to find . . ." He paused, unable to remember.

Connie pointed at the dollhouse. "Well, here's Lou's object."

Jason flinched. "Oh, right. But we can't smash it to pieces while they're all still inside. Can we?"

"I think not." She went on, "Then there's Cal's camera. Nina's cloak. Rufus's sketchbook."

"What about Marcus?"

"Marcus didn't come to Larkspur with an object," said Connie. "None of his group did."

"Oh, yeah." Jason sighed. "But then . . . how do we get him out of Larkspur?"

"We'll worry about that when the time comes," said Connie.

CHAPTER 26

IN THE BALLROOM, the kids paused to regroup.

The ceilings soared twenty feet high. Chandeliers the size of small cars hung from velvet-covered chains, casting the brightest light any of them had seen inside Larkspur House thus far.

Lou was thankful for it. After everything they'd just run from—the refrigerator tunnel, the haunted dog kennel—they all needed a moment of respite. What frightened her, however, was the question of why the house would allow them to have it.

They sat huddled in the center of the room, the rotting goop from the refrigerator beginning to crust on their skin and clothes. Too bad the stench was as strong as ever. "I feel like this won't ever wash off," said Cal.

"Don't say that!" Nina exclaimed. "Ew!"

As the others talked about Sadie and the ukulele, Lou found herself glancing around, expecting another horror to burst through the closed doors and stampede through their temporary sanctuary.

"What do you think, Lou?" Rufus was staring at her, wearing a hopeful smile. He held his arm where the shadow-dogs had bitten him. A red welt had formed, but thankfully, they hadn't drawn blood. "If we track our Larkspur objects down and smash them, like Sadie's ukulele, maybe we'll all get to go home too."

"And not only that," Cal added, "but maybe every time one of us leaves, another part of the house will fall down. We'll be free, and the creature will be defeated."

Marcus watched Lou, looking worried that she might break into pieces like the part of the house they'd run from.

"What about you, Marcus?" Lou asked. "Do you have an object to destroy?"

He shook his head. "Don't worry about me. I'll come up with something."

Lou's mouth was dry and gritty. The thought of creeping through the house, searching for their little haunted treasures, made her nauseated, but she didn't see any other way out. "How do we get started?" she asked.

"Maybe your brother can help us again," said Rufus, standing and walking to a far wall, where a line of tall windows was covered by heavy curtains.

"My brother?" Lou's voice squeaked. She knew that Rufus and Nina believed the reflection they'd seen throughout the house had really been Jason. Deep down, she still worried it was a trick of the creature. But Rufus didn't have a chance to answer. When he pulled back the curtains, he found a wall covered with peacock-green wallpaper. He dragged the next curtain aside, only to discover the same. Down the line he went, groaning louder with every discovery.

"There should be windows there," said Lou.

"The house knew what we needed," said Cal. "So it removed them."

"We're on our own?" Rufus asked, his voice echoing off the high ceilings.

Marcus blinked. "We've been on our own for a while now."

"Not so fast," said Nina. "Look." She pointed at her feet. Lou had thought Nina had been so distraught by what had happened earlier that she'd started to withdraw into her own head. But it wasn't the case. Staring up from the glossy floor was the reflection of her brother. He was accompanied by a girl in a black dress and white apron whom Lou didn't recognize.

Lou hopped away, worrying that the boy might reach up through the floor, grab her ankle, and then pull her down. But she looked into his eyes and found that he was looking back. There was no menace in his face as there had been when she'd seen him on the movie screen. The girl smiled sadly and then waved. "It's him," Lou whispered. "It's Jason. He's really here with me." Her breath hitched, but she wouldn't allow herself to cry in front of everyone. Instead, she crouched down and reached out to the glossy reflection.

To her surprise, Jason reached back. Extending his fore-finger, they connected. It felt like she could almost feel his heart beating. Through the reflection, Lou watched a tear splash onto the floor below, and she wondered if her brother noticed. Jason dragged his finger along the wood, and Lou mirrored him. He was . . . writing something. Lou's finger smudged against the gloss, letter after letter after letter.

Nina read aloud from over Lou's shoulder. "Camera, cloak, sketchbook . . . dollhouse." Her voice rose as she realized what he was doing. "Keep going."

Rufus rushed back from the curtains to where the group was crouched around the writing.

Jason and Lou continued, marking more letters onto the floor. They moved as one, their shoulders twisting, their spines wavering, their skulls swiveling as if in an awkward dance.

1. *Master bedroom*
2. *Observatory*
3. *Library*

They stared at the message for a moment, trying to figure out what it meant.

"We all arrived in different parts of the house earlier today," said Rufus once the siblings had slowed. "Does anyone remember seeing any of these places while wandering?"

Lou watched as Jason continued to write out: *Lou, Marcus has a book* . . .

"Marcus, you've been here the longest," Nina said. "Any clue?"

Before Marcus could answer, Cal leapt to his feet. Without looking back, he raced toward the ballroom door.

"Cal!" Marcus called out. "It's not safe out there on your own! Wait for the rest of us!" He was up and running, and within seconds, he too had disappeared into the hallway.

CHAPTER 27

LOU, NINA, AND Rufus glanced at one another, stunned. Then they raced from the ballroom and barreled out into the hall.

Footsteps echoed from their right, so that's the direction they ran. When they reached a wide part of the hall where the ceiling arched, meeting in sturdy wooden rafters, they paused to gain their bearings.

Marcus's voice came from the top of a tall staircase. "Cal, wait! We need to stick together!"

"What the heck is Cal doing?" asked Nina, taking the steps two by two.

"He's probably trying to help," said Rufus, moving more slowly behind her. Lou followed at the rear.

"Well, he's *not* helping." Nina stopped ahead and turned back, as if to address all of the grand hall behind her. "He's putting the rest of us in danger. We finally have a clue how to get out of this horrid place and he's ruining it!"

"Shh," Lou whispered. "We shouldn't draw attention to ourselves."

"Don't shush me," Nina spat. "I'm not a child."

Lou kept her voice low and soft as she answered. "Technically, we're *all* children. Unless you're a very young-looking thirty-year-old."

Nina didn't think the joke was funny. She scoffed and folded her arms, waiting for them to reach the step on which she stood. "I'll bet Cal is heading to the first place your brother wrote on the floor. The master bedroom." She waved for them to follow her up the rest of the stairs. "I think Rufus and I passed it earlier when your brother and that girl were using the mirrors to lead us to the kitchen." She lowered her voice and added, "I'm sorry for snapping at you guys. Being angry is easier than feeling scared."

Lou and Rufus made eye contact, but didn't say a word.

When they reached the landing, they listened for a clue—a footfall, a sneeze, a cry—telling where the other boys had gone. Nina led the way down a hallway with bloodred wallpaper.

"I'm scared too," Lou said. Nina exhaled through her nose, but didn't answer. It was clear that she was fighting something inside her head.

Rufus walked slightly behind the two girls. "I have a method to stop myself from getting scared. It's foolproof actually."

"Tell us," said Lou, trying to keep up with Nina.

"Well, it's sort of embarrassing," said Rufus. "But back home in Kansas, I created a secret identity."

Lou chirped out laughter, then covered her mouth, hoping she didn't offend him. But Rufus only smiled wider.

Even Nina slowed and turned to look back. "A secret identity?"

Rufus shrugged. "Middle school has been a nightmare for me. Sorta like this house. People have called me names. They make fun of my size, of my accent—"

"You don't have an accent," said Nina.

"I've tried to get rid of it so the jerks quit teasing me. But at home, me and my parents speak Tagalog all the time."

Nina nodded, as if she understood.

"Anyway, I love reading comic books," said Rufus. "Miles Morales is *the best* Spider-Man. I wish I could sling webs in New York City. And Captain America is my favorite superhero. Strong and brave and handsome." He began to whisper.

"*My* secret identity is based on a different kind of power. I call myself The Sneak."

"The Sneak?" Nina squeaked.

"Yeah! And I've figured out how to use his power in real life. I can walk through the halls of my school like I'm totally invisible. Close my locker so it makes no sound. Sit in the back of the class and duck down just far enough to never be called on."

"It sucks that you have to do that," said Lou. "No one should feel invisible."

"It's easier than what my father wanted me to do. Stand up to the bullies. Fight back. I tried his way for half a day and came home with a black eye and a split lip."

The house rumbled suddenly, and the floor trembled for several seconds. The three froze, then glanced around as if something were about to come dashing out of the shadows at them. Lou waited for the boys to cry out, but after a moment, silence settled again.

"I love the idea of The Sneak," Nina whispered after a moment. "Teach me how to do it."

"Me too!" Lou said quietly.

Rufus beamed. As they continued after Cal and Marcus, he showed them his techniques. "First, you have to learn where to step. Certain spots are squeakier than others." He pressed his foot onto several spots on the floor, all of which let out a small squeal. He sighed. "This may not be the best place to practice. Next, you train yourself to hold your breath for a long time. When you're hiding from someone, you don't want a sniffly nose to give you away."

Shouting echoed from down the hallway, bringing the house back into sharp focus. "Help me!" The voice belonged to Cal, and it trembled as if he were in pain.

Lou, Nina, and Rufus raced to the door at the far end of the hallway. Inside, they discovered Cal and Marcus standing side by side next to a four-poster canopy bed.

The master bedroom. They'd made it!

"What's wrong, Cal?" Lou called out. Cal grimaced. That was when Lou noticed that Marcus was gripping Cal's skin behind his neck. "Marcus, *what are you doing?*"

Marcus stared at Cal, tightening his grip, rattling him slightly. "How about I let Cal answer that question?"

"I wasn't doing anything!" Cal answered. As soon as he said it, Lou had a feeling it wasn't true.

"Tell them, Cal," said Marcus. "What were you trying to do?" Lou didn't know what to say or what to do. Something had come over her cousin. He looked angry and sad, but also resigned. "No? Okay then. I'll say it. After I chased Cal in here, I found him trying to hide something underneath the mattress."

Marcus used his free hand to point at an empty cage attached to the wall beside a tall wooden dresser. The black iron bars were similar to the ones they'd seen down in the music room that had contained Sadie's ukulele.

"What was it?" Nina asked. "What were you hiding under the mattress, Cal?" She sounded shaky, as if she knew the answer but wished she didn't. Lou stared at the empty cage, wondering which of their items would have been easy enough to slip out through the bars. "Please tell me it wasn't my cloak," Nina finished, her brow furrowed.

"It *was* your cloak," Marcus said.

Rufus twitched. "But if the cloak is under the mattress, how can Nina destroy it? Wasn't that the plan, Cal? We find the objects, we bust them up, we go home?"

Lou stepped toward the boys. "Cal?" She sounded very small, like a miniature version of herself. "Can you explain yourself?"

Cal looked back at them, fear in his eyes, and then nodded.

CHAPTER 28

"I DID IT to help the group," Cal said, his voice choked.

Marcus was still holding his neck, refusing to ease his grip.

Nina shook her head. "How would hiding my cloak help the group?"

Cal swallowed nervously. "In horror movies, there's usually a betrayal." The group was shocked into a momentary hush.

Rufus proceeded cautiously, as if any word he spoke might set off a chain reaction of explosions. "And *you* decided to fill that role?" Cal groaned, and they all took it as a *yes*. "Because you were afraid that if you weren't the betrayer first, you'd end up as the betrayed?"

Cal burst into tears. "I'm sorry!" he cried out. "Marcus, let me go, please." Cal arched his back and tried to twist away.

"I'm confused," Nina said. "How was cheating me supposed to *help the group*?" She finished with air quotes.

Cal struggled to speak again. "Because . . . because if one of us were left behind . . . stuck here in the house . . . the creature might leave the rest of us alone. If we gave it at least *part* of what it wants, the rest of us might be safe."

Nina's breath grew rapid as she stared at Cal, her rage blooming like a slow-motion bomb. "And you decided that *I'd* be the one left behind?!"

"It wasn't personal," said Cal. "It's just that . . . this room was closest."

"So then, in your mind, any of us would have been fair game?" asked Rufus. "A sacrifice to save yourself?"

"I'm sorry." Cal coughed and sputtered. "But we're *inside* a scary story. It's supposed to work this way."

"This is not a story," Lou said. "This is our lives. We are *human beings*. You had no right. You don't get to choose what happens to any of us." Her throat swelled as she fought to keep down her anger. "There would only have been a betrayal if one of us had decided to do what you did." Memories of her parents' arguments rattled inside her skull. "It wasn't fate. It was your *choice*, jerk-wad."

Marcus nodded slightly. Cal tried again to squirm out of his grip, but Marcus squeezed his neck so hard he dropped to the floor and landed on his knees. Marcus squatted and grabbed his collar. Cal covered his face with his hands and sobbed.

"You're right, Lou," Marcus whispered. "But you're also wrong. There *was* always going to be a betrayal here. It just wasn't supposed to be Cal who did it." Cal became still. He turned his head to look up at Marcus, confused. Marcus smiled down at him, lips pressed tightly, concealing his teeth. Lou shuddered. What was Marcus hiding? "It was *always* going to be me."

"Funny joke," said Rufus, forcing a laugh. "You got him back, Marcus. Good one. Let's grab Nina's cloak and do what we came here to do."

Marcus shook his head. "I'm not joking."

"You've made your point, Marcus," said Lou. "Let him go."

Looking away from her, Marcus added, "It's not up to me to let *any* of you go."

His words hit the group like a blast of bitter cold. Lou, Nina, and Rufus stiffened, their mouths open in shock. Cal tried to scramble up to his feet, but Marcus raised his foot and then pressed him back to the ground.

"Oww!" Cal squawked. "What do you think you're doing, you *psycho*?"

"Holding you in place," said Marcus. Then, with his other foot, he jumped up and down, pounding on the bedroom floor, as if signaling to someone.

Or something.

A rumble belched out from the wide space beneath the long bed. All the color drained from Cal's face. He swiveled to peer under the frame, and a look of panic sprang into his eyes. He fought to push himself up and away from Marcus, but the other boy only leaned harder onto his spine.

"Marcus!" Lou cried out. "Quit it!"

The rumbling morphed into a groan, a long, drawn-out chuckle—a breathy, crunchy noise, like footsteps on gravel. Marcus shoved Cal closer to the space beneath the mattress. Cal rolled, unable to stop himself. The chuckling transformed into deeper, vibrant laughter.

Lou wanted to run forward, to pull Cal out of the way, but two gigantic hands emerged from the darkness. The white skin that clung to its fingers was transparent, and Lou could see a mess of bones and twigs and tendon and twine moving within, as if the thing had built itself from scraps it had found lying around the house. Long arms followed, scuttling along the floor behind the hands.

Marcus leapt backward in awe. Cal released a shriek so loud that the whole room seemed to shiver with pleasure. With a snap, the arms recoiled back underneath the bed. Cal was gone, but his screaming lingered. Lou covered her ears, but she couldn't drown out the sounds.

The silence that followed was more terrifying than anything she'd just seen and heard.

There was a fluttering in her stomach, a feeling she'd never experienced before. Lou sprang toward Marcus, her fists raised, her teeth bared, but her cousin saw her coming. His expression was empty. Dead. He spun and bolted toward a door that appeared in the opposite wall. Flinging himself through, he pulled the door shut behind him. Lou grappled with the knob, but when she managed to rip the door open again, she found herself staring at a wall. The doorknob dropped from her grip and rolled across the floor.

"No!" She slammed her palms against the new barrier and screamed, "Marcus, come back! What did you do to Cal?!" Finally, she turned back to her friends, wiping at her cheeks.

Rufus approached the canopy bed, keeping a careful distance, far from where the giant hands had snatched Cal. Still crying, he crouched and peered into the space where Cal had disappeared. He let out a choking sound and then glanced up at the girls. "He's gone," he whispered. "There's nothing here."

Nina shivered and rubbed at her arms. She moved toward the bed.

"Don't get too close," said Rufus.

Ignoring his advice, she inched past him to the mattress, pausing with every step. "Still nothing there?" she asked. Rufus glanced again and nodded. She shoved her hands between the bed's mattress and frame and dug around. Seconds later, she tugged her black cloak out from where Cal had hidden it and bolted away from the dark space under the frame.

Lou watched as Nina stared down at the object in her hands. Her eyes were filled with fear, and she threw the cloak to the floor. "Is he dead?" Nina asked the others. "Did it kill him?"

Lou didn't want to think about it. She looked around the room for anything that might be reflective. The floor. The windows. But everything had taken on a dull opaque sheen. Still she called out, "Jason! If you're there, please help us!"

CHAPTER 29

JASON AND CONNIE watched it all happen from outside of the house. The bedroom windows went fuzzy, and he started screaming, "Bring me back inside! I need to help Lou!"

But Connie blinked, unaffected. "I won't. Not when you're like this. Remember what happened last time you drew attention to yourself? You ended up way out there." Connie looked to the darkness.

"But Lou needs me." His voice broke. "Marcus . . . Marcus might hurt her."

Connie was controlled, her tone even, as if she'd seen it all before. And she had. "Remember what you wanted to tell your sister earlier?" she asked. "The only way to stop the creature that lives in this place is to control your fear. What you're doing now is only going to make it stronger. Look." She nodded at the part of the house that had crumbled when Sadie had gone home. The foundation had already re-formed, and the walls had appeared again. "A direct result of what just happened. The house knew that you and the others figured out a way to beat it. It got rid of Cal, knowing how that would affect all of you. Now it's using your new fear to give itself life. This is exactly what my father's society wanted to have happen when they marked those objects with the cursed symbols. We mustn't fall for the trap."

Jason took a deep breath, trying to find a quiet spot inside his head—somewhere he could hide from his worry. But it was as if his brain had taken away all the secret and safe memories that he usually depended on. All he could think of were his parents fighting about . . .

1. *Money*
2. *Blaming each other for stupid stuff*
3. *Lou's nightmares . . .*

He needed to get Connie to see that he was calm. "Why did Marcus do it?" he asked. "I don't buy Cal's horror-movie explanation. Is my cousin evil? Did the house force him? Or was Marcus paying Cal back for betraying Nina?"

Connie stared at him, as if he were a book she were trying to read as pages kept turning on her. "I don't know what Marcus was doing. I don't know why he's still at Larkspur while the others he came with are—"

"Jason!" A voice was calling to him from inside the house.

It was Lou.

Instinct made him tense up again, but Jason knew that Connie would only be angry with him if he flipped out. "She needs me," he said quietly. "You know it's true. Or you wouldn't have brought me here in the first place."

Connie smiled sadly and then nodded. She held out her hands to him. But before Jason could take them, movement blurred the darkness behind her. A pale face appeared. Dark eyes and red curly hair.

"Marcus," Jason whispered. "How did you get out here?"

Marcus grabbed Connie's arms as she started to turn and pinned them behind her back. Connie wriggled, trying to get away, but Marcus only tightened his grip.

Marcus called out into the void, his face a mask of fear. "I did what you asked! Why aren't you keeping your side of the bargain?!"

"Who are you talking to?"

"Who do you think?" Marcus spat.

For a moment, Jason's vision went white with rage. "Why are you doing this? We're family!"

"The longer you stay at Larkspur House," said Marcus, "the less that will mean to you."

Jason shook his head. "I don't understand. How could you do what you did to that boy? To Cal? How can you hurt Connie? Can't you see she's in pain?"

Marcus's voice wobbled as if he might burst into tears. "You have no idea what I've been through. The things I've seen here." He shook his head, as if trying to block out images that flickered through his mind. "I would have given anything to leave. But the house wouldn't let me. Not until others arrived. The creature spoke. It told me it would grant my freedom if I helped 'scare' the new victims. So that's what I did. But now . . . Now it's not giving me my reward."

"*Poor you*," said Jason.

Marcus tightened his grip on Connie. She winced. "You should be thankful I chose Cal instead of Louise."

Jason's face burned. Electricity shot through his limbs. "*Thankful?*" he repeated with disgust. "You should be worried that I don't tear your *lips* off!"

Marcus's eyes were dull, lifeless, as if his soul were out wandering the wastelands in the distance. "*You* weren't supposed to be here at all, Jason. But Connie . . . *Helpful*

Connie . . . just couldn't resist. The creature told me that she has a tendency to stick her nose where it doesn't belong." He called out to the void again. "Is *she* the one you wanted? What if I bring her to you? Then will you let me go?"

Connie's wide eyes latched on to Jason's. Her pale face looked like it was made of porcelain, like it might simply shatter. Jason recalled what she'd said earlier, about how she wouldn't leave Larkspur until she was certain it was dead. She'd be its watchdog—a protector of the innocents. For the first time, Jason truly understood what that meant. She was a hero. His cousin would not be her undoing. He stepped toward Marcus, fists clenched.

Connie shook her head. Marcus squeezed her tighter. It was all Jason could take. He lunged for his cousin, but Marcus was too quick. He spun away before Jason could make contact.

Marcus dragged Connie from the dollhouse and into the shadows. Jason was about to chase them when Connie called out, "Stay with your sister! Help Louise!"

CHAPTER 30

JASON STEPPED OUT of the halo of light that came from the dollhouse. He heard the sounds of creatures moving through the darkness nearby. Scaly tails slithering. Enamel claws digging into the ground. They must have been drawn by the arguing. He strained to hear Connie, but she was gone.

"Jason, help me!" Lou called out again.

Maybe Marcus had *wanted* him to give chase. Jason wouldn't have come back. Lou would have been left alone with the last two kids—Nina and Rufus—and who knew if either of them were trustworthy anymore?

He had to find a way back inside the dollhouse. But Connie was the one who'd known the way in and out.

He slowed his breath and concentrated. Over the past few hours, he'd watched Connie work her own kind of magic. He thought of the book she'd taken from the shelf in her father's art studio—how she'd stood in front of the mirror and closed her eyes, trying to will the book into the pocket of her apron.

He closed his eyes and faced the house.

"Jason! *Please!*" Lou's voice echoed faintly out into the gloom.

He focused on Lou, picturing the room where he'd last seen her. He imagined all the details he could remember.

1. *The blue of the wallpaper*
2. *The curve of the canopy bed*
3. *The soaring height of the ceiling*

He thought of the few times back home in the condo that Lou had asked him to help her put together a piece of miniature furniture for her dollhouse. He'd never admitted to her how much he'd enjoyed it. But it wasn't so different from thinking about the maps he'd drawn of Mount Diablo and the ecosystems that thrived there. The building had been like a three-dimensional plan of a place that neither of them could have imagined truly existed.

The air felt suddenly different against his skin. Drier. Cooler. He opened his eyes to find himself standing inside the master bedroom. Nina and Rufus were only a few feet away. Lou was hunched over, kneeling by his feet.

He'd done it! He'd made it back inside. By himself!

"Jason!" Lou called out again. She still could not see him. He sat beside her and wrapped his arms around her, but it wasn't like a real hug. Where their bodies should have connected, Jason felt an immense gulf. He could not feel her warmth, and he didn't believe she could feel his either. Yet she seemed to calm, relaxing her shoulders. "Jason?" she whispered.

"I'm here," he replied. She couldn't hear him, couldn't see him, but he *knew* she sensed his presence. Maybe that was enough?

Rufus and Nina had left the black cloak lying on the floor several feet away and were scouring the bedroom for a tool with which they could destroy it. Rufus dragged open the drawers of a wardrobe between the windows, and Nina pawed through the cabinets of a vanity. Something shiny on the floor near the baseboard caught Jason's attention. A pair of scissors. He leaned over and whispered its location into Lou's ear.

To his surprise, she flinched and turned. *Jason?* she mouthed, almost looking into his eyes. In that moment, he was certain she'd seen him. "I'm here," he said again. A glimmer shone in her face. A knowledge that he'd been with her all along.

Wiping at her cheeks, Lou approached the object and picked it up. "Will this help?" she asked Nina.

"I hope so." Nina brandished the scissors.

Rufus joined the girls. The three encircled the cloak as Jason stood unseen a few inches away. Nina reached out to the black velvet, but when she got close, the fabric bunched up and moved from her hand. Nina gasped. "Did you guys see that?"

"It moved," said Rufus.

"How?" asked Lou.

"It doesn't matter," said Nina. "It won't be moving again."

As if to prove her wrong, the cloak slid toward her. Nina shrieked and dropped the scissors. The cloak reached up across her torso to her neck, twisting itself into a ropelike shape and then looping around her throat. Rufus and Lou both pulled at the cloak's hem, but it only jerked Nina forward.

"Oh, no!" Jason breathed.

The cloak tightened around Nina's neck, and a gurgling noise escaped her throat. Her eyes rolled back in her head, bulging like marbles.

Rufus attacked the noose. He slipped his fingers between it and Nina's skin, but as he tried to pry it away, the loop only grew tighter.

Lou swept her hands across the floor, and the scissors clattered. She jumped on them, then spun toward the cloak. The fabric rippled as she cut into the spot that was closest to her.

The noose loosened, and Nina tore it away from herself. She fell to the floor, coughing and sputtering. Rufus crouched at her side and rubbed at her back. "Are you okay?" he asked, but Nina couldn't answer.

Lou continued to cut at the cloak, but the scissors were too small to do much damage.

"Tear it up," Jason whispered. "Come on, Lou."

The fabric slid across the floor, heading for Nina again. She glanced up just in time, rolled aside, and then grabbed at the spot where Lou had cut into the cloak. Sitting up, Nina clutched at it and then brought her hands swiftly apart.

A shredding sound echoed across the room like a shriek.

A moment later, Lou and Rufus pounced on the cloak. They both grabbed handfuls of it and then threw themselves in opposite directions. The cloak ripped in half, and then fluttered to the floor lifelessly.

Nina, Lou, Rufus, and Jason stared at it, waiting for it to do something more—stitch itself back together, or maybe rise up into two different pieces, equally strong and equally angry. But all that happened was a slight tremor that rattled the room.

Then Nina let out a cry. "I can see my house!" she said, glancing around. "I think I'm going home too!" Her eyes appeared to be focused on what the others couldn't see. Her mom? Her aunt? Briefly, Jason imagined Connie out in the darkness. He sidled up to Lou and watched as Nina become a dim version of the girl they'd briefly known. "Thank you all," she said before fading away.

A massive jolt rocked the master bedroom, and Lou and Rufus stumbled into each other as the canopy bed shuddered across the floor.

CHAPTER 31

GRAY BLOTCHES APPEARED on the walls and spread rapidly, like ink on tissue paper, reaching up to the ceiling and down to the floor. The rot chased Lou and Rufus as they raced for the bedroom door, Jason right behind them.

In the hall, he stepped ahead. "This way!" Jason called out. Lou and Rufus followed as if they'd heard him. The group ran as one.

The house rattled and roared. Lou stumbled and cried out. Jason went to catch her, but his hand bounced off her body. Rufus pulled her up, and they all kept running. Recalling the floor plan of the dollhouse, Jason raced down passages and around corners until he was certain that they were far from the collapsing wing.

Soon, the sounds of destruction quieted behind them, and silence throbbed in his ears. Looking around, he noticed they were in a gallery space on the second floor. More creepy portraits of Connie's father stared out from the walls, but there were no windows. No glass through which the others could see Jason.

Lou sat down, wheezing. Rufus glanced back in the direction they'd come from. "Are we safe here?" he asked.

"No," Lou said softly. "We're not safe anywhere."

"It's just the two of us now."

Lou nodded. Jason knelt beside her. He held his hand several inches over her own, trying to feel the warmth of her skin. Then Lou added, "We're not alone. Can you feel it? My brother is here too."

Rufus inclined his head. "He wants to help. Just like before. You trust him now?"

"I do," Lou said, glancing at Rufus. "I feel him like a memory of a voice in my head." She sighed. "Jason told us before where we needed to go in order to find the last of our objects. We've got to destroy them before the creature can refocus."

"Which way?" asked Rufus.

Jason blinked, concentrating on Cal's camera. A moment later, he stood and walked toward a doorway at the gallery's far wall.

Lou stood too, holding out her arm. "He wants us to go this way."

Rufus smiled. He raised his eyebrows, and his face changed slightly. He wore a glimmer of excitement. "Tell your brother: It's time to *Sneak*."

CHAPTER 32

JASON CREPT THROUGH countless open doorways, and Lou followed silently with Rufus at her side, as if they were all tethered together.

Rufus moved with spy-like skill. If Jason didn't turn back every few steps, he might have thought that the boy had left him and his sister to wander the house alone. He wondered if the house, or the creature, or *whatever* was in charge here, could sense him like his sister could.

They reached an archway off a long hall that opened onto a balcony. Connie's father must have gazed at constellations out here, gathering inspiration for his landscape paintings. *The Observatory*. An antique telescope was pointed toward what should have been star-spangled heavens. Instead it stared out a blackness one might discover in the depths of a fathomless cave.

Lou and Rufus peered at the iron cage that was bolted to a dark corner on the floor.

Inside the cage was an accordion camera—the one that Cal had found in the woods of Greencliffe.

"Shoot," whispered Rufus. "How are we supposed to get it out of there?"

"We're not," Lou answered. She grabbed the telescope and folded up the tripod, then pushed the legs between the bars of the cage. Using all of her strength, she jabbed the tripod into the cage, smashing into the camera. It felt like she was killing something. Her arm shook. The balcony shivered. Lou hit the camera over and over until it was nothing but a small pile of broken glass and crumpled metal. If Cal were still at Larkspur—and Lou was pretty sure he wasn't—now would have been when he would have vanished.

Instead, the building echoed the smashing of the camera with a destruction all its own. A crack raced across the doorway back inside, and the balcony floor tilted away from the house.

Rufus leapt across the gap and then reached back for Lou, grasping her forearms just before she lost her balance. The balcony fell away into the darkness as Lou slammed against the wall just below the doorway. Rufus grunted and groaned, pulling her up to safety.

As she scrambled to stand up, she found that a gray patch had already spread out underneath her feet and was racing ahead of them into the hallway. The floor felt soft, as if it might crumble away at any moment.

Lou clutched Rufus's hand, and together they dashed at the advancing line of decay, hopping over it and continuing on toward the final cursed objects.

The house stopped trembling when Lou and Rufus reached a room filled with books. Shelves lined an entire wall from floor to ceiling, hundreds of volumes packed densely between them.

"This is it," said Rufus. "The library."

"Your sketchbook must be here." Lou scanned the room. A large portrait of a girl with intense eyes stared out at her from above a fireplace mantel. It was the same girl she'd seen reflected in the ballroom's floor. *Was she holding a book?* As Lou stepped toward the painting, a spark snapped inside the small pile of logs within the mouth of the fireplace and soon it was engulfed with flame. "It must think we're still playing that old game. Nice try, *House*," she said, glancing back at

Rufus. She expected him to return a grin, or at least a smirk, but he wasn't even looking at her. He faced the shelves, his spine rigid, as if under a spell.

She peered at him and saw a disturbing emptiness in his gaze. He was staring at the rows of books, his jaw slack. "Rufus?" she asked, but he didn't respond. "What's wrong? Did you see something scary?"

She extended her hand to shake his shoulder, but before she could, voices caught her attention. They sounded like her family. They were coming from the wall of books, and she couldn't make out what they were saying. She found herself stepping toward the shelves, pressing her ear against a well-worn leather volume. The voices went on, as if from inside the book itself.

No . . . not inside the *book* . . .

Lou flicked the tome from the shelf, and bright light beamed out from the space where it had been sitting—a shaft of illumination like morning sunlight through a crack in a curtain.

She peered through and saw what looked like the kitchen of the Benjamin family's condo in Walnut Creek.

CHAPTER 33

LOU'S BROTHER AND mother and father were eating breakfast at the kitchen table.

Home! she thought. *I'm almost there! It's right on the other side of this bookcase . . .*

"How did you sleep, honey?" Mom asked Jason.

Jason's smile was too wide. "Awesomely."

Dad nudged his shoulder playfully. "That's the best news I've heard all morning, kiddo." He and Mom laughed hard, as if it were the funniest joke he'd ever made. Something seemed off.

Lou flipped a few more books out of her way, making the space on the shelf wider. She wondered if she could crawl through. "Hey!" she called to them. "Here I am! Jason!"

Everyone ignored her.

"The past few days have been so quiet," said Mom, glancing down the hall toward Lou's room. "Thank goodness your sister is finally gone."

Lou's scalp went prickly with surprise. Was that a joke?

"I thought she'd never leave," said Dad.

Jason nodded. "I was sure she'd eventually sleepwalk away from us. What an annoying little bug she was."

Lou shook her head. "You're not my family," she whispered, if only to herself. "My brother is with me here."

The boy's eyes flashed amber, and chills danced across Lou's skin. "I like the new Louise much better," he went on, talking to his mother. "Not a peep all night."

New Louise?

"I should bring her to the table," said the man who looked like her father. He stood and pulled away the fourth chair. Then he disappeared into the hall. A few seconds later, he returned. In his arms was a figure that looked just like Lou. It wore her white nightgown. Dark hair obscured its features.

After a moment, Lou saw that it wasn't real hair but tangles of thick yarn.

The man who looked like her father placed the life-size doll in Lou's chair.

"Good morning, New Louise," said the woman who looked like her mother. "How did you sleep?" She waited for a moment, as if she expected the doll to answer. "Oh, that's right. You're *still* asleep. You'll always be asleep now." Lou realized that the woman was now talking to her directly, taunting. All of them were. Jason and Dad too. "Much easier this way. For all of us." The family chortled as Lou's jaw dropped.

When the doll turned its head, its stitched eyes glaring, Lou finally found her voice. It gushed from her mouth in a scream of horror and didn't stop, not even when Lou ran out of breath.

Jason paced several steps away from Lou and Rufus as they stared up at the bookshelves.

He tried to touch Lou's arm, but before he could make contact, the room changed entirely. He was back home in the condo's kitchen. A nightmare version of himself and the rest of his family were sitting in the dining nook and laughing so hard, they'd all turned blue. In Lou's chair, there was a life-size version of the doll that had taken his sister's place when he'd opened the dollhouse earlier.

Lou was cowering in a shadowy corner of the kitchen. She'd covered her face with her hands. When he reached out to take them away, Lou surprised him by yelping. He'd touched her! She blinked at him with frightened eyes and then jerked away.

"It's me," he said, keeping his voice low so he didn't scare her. "I'm here with you." Lou's gaze flittered past him toward the maniacal laughter. "They're fake. A bad dream. But *I'm* real, Lou. I'm here to help you. I've been with you since the beginning."

Lou grew still, then swallowed and winced, as if grit were stuck in her throat. "Are we home?"

"No. We're still inside the dollhouse. You need to find the last of the cursed objects. The creature is inside your head, trying to stop you. You've got to tear through the books back in the library to reach the cage."

"How do I snap out of it?"

The laughter grew louder behind him. He heard footsteps coming toward them. Lou whimpered.

Jason thought about Connie's abilities—about how he'd found his way back into the house once Marcus had dragged her away. "Close your eyes. Block out the noise. It's not real."

"How do you know?"

He squeezed at her fingers and felt the warmth of her skin. "Because I can finally hold your hand. And you feel more real than anything else in this horrible place."

The roaring halted, and the room went quiet.

They were no longer in the kitchen.

Flames flickered in the library's fireplace. Connie's portrait stared down at them from the wall above it. The shelves of books towered overhead.

Lou stumbled backward, returning to her body. She spun, searching for him. Jason tried to take her hand again but the barrier had returned. She zeroed in on Rufus, who was still standing frozen before the bookcase. "Rufus! Wake up!" When he didn't respond, she shoved at his shoulder.

"Whoa!" he cried out, taking in the room. "What happened? I was just . . ." He shuddered. Lou hoped he didn't tell her what he'd seen. She didn't want more scary images floating around in her head. "Was it a dream?"

Lou nodded. "I was stuck in one too. My brother rescued me. He says the creature wants to distract us. We must be close to getting out of here for good." Sweeping her arm across one of the shelves, she brought a pile of books crashing to the floor. Rufus looked at her like she'd lost what was left of her mind. "The cage is hidden here. Help me clear all of this away."

Jason watched as Lou and Rufus pulled the shelves apart, tossing books and searching for the cage.

"There!" Rufus pointed.

A few feet over their heads, resting inside a pocket of the wall, there was a small, red, clothbound sketchbook. It was blocked by the familiar grid of iron bars.

"Can you reach it?" Lou asked.

Rufus climbed the rickety shelves like rungs of a ladder. The shelf creaked, pulling away from the wall.

"Careful."

He shoved his hand through the bars and grabbed the book. But it was too wide to fit through. "I can't get it out."

"There's got to be a way," said Lou, stepping back, trying to get a better glimpse of the book. "We were able to reach all the other objects."

Jason whispered to himself, "Think of it as a puzzle."

"Think of it as a puzzle," Lou echoed.

Jason flinched. Had she heard him?

"The camera was stuck just like my sketchbook," said Rufus. "You smashed it from the outside."

Lou's eyes lit up. "Exactly."

Rufus smiled. He reached back through the bars and flipped open the book cover. Snatching a handful of pages, he tore them from the binding and tossed them to the floor.

"Yes!" Lou yelled triumphantly. She pounced on the crumpled pages. Each page was filled with sketches of the man who'd built this house. His distorted face stared up at her. It was the same face she'd seen in various frames hanging throughout the halls. Racing across the room to the roaring fire, Lou threw the paper onto the blaze.

Seconds later, Rufus jumped down from his perch on the shelves. He followed Lou to the fireplace and tossed the rest of the pages in. They grew bright before turning black.

Seconds later, Rufus was a blur in Lou's vision. He held out his arms to give her a hug. As she grasped his middle, he faded away just like the others, and Lou ended up squeezing herself.

Opening her eyes, Lou took off before the tremors began again.

CHAPTER 34

DARKNESS WHIPPED AROUND her. Her lungs ached from running.

Lou had turned so many corners—had ducked through so many doorways—she no longer knew which section of the house she was in.

She stopped when she felt her brother's presence leave her.

"Jason?" she called out, hoping he might answer her like he'd done during the horrid vision of the doll in the kitchen. But there was no answer.

Looking around, she found that she was standing in a vast nothingness, all alone. She needed to destroy the dollhouse to free herself from its grasp, but how could she do anything if the place no longer existed?

Somewhere close by, she heard a vague muttering. "Jason?" A dark voice in her head sounded out dim words. *He left you here. They all left you here. There is no way out now.*

Lou hunkered down, her scalp tingling. Covering her ears, she tried to do what Jason had told her earlier. *Block out the noise. Concentrate on breathing.*

The dark voice continued, *Wake up. You're dreaming again. All you have to do is open your eyes.*

Lou gritted her teeth and yelled out, "Shut up, shut up, shut up!"

But more voices rose like a storm inside her head, spinning her thoughts until she wasn't sure what was real or what was a nightmare.

Jason had been following his sister closely when she paused suddenly in the middle of the foyer. She spun around with her arms out, as if she weren't sure of her balance, then called out to him. All of a sudden she slumped to the floor, unconscious.

"Lou!" He tried to place his hands on her shoulders, but the magnetic barrier kept them separated. "Wake up. You're dreaming again. All you have to do is open your eyes." But she didn't move.

Her head was lying at an odd angle on the wooden floor.

He tried to lift it, to rest it on his lap, but it was like attempting to bend a marble statue. "Lou, please!"

Her skin paled to an ashy gray, and her eyes seemed to sink into their sockets. If the house was attacking her as it had back in the library, she must be trapped inside another horrifying vision. The evil that lived here was using her fear to save itself. Her cheekbones protruded, as if something were draining her life away.

"No!" Jason cried out. He attempted to place his palm on her forehead, to gain access to her mind, but it didn't work this time. Something invisible smacked at his hand, and he clutched it to his chest for a moment.

Holding it up, he saw several red lines across his skin where claws had scraped him.

If he couldn't reach Lou through her thoughts, there was only one other way to save her.

Destroy the dollhouse.

But they were still trapped inside! He wondered where Connie was. She'd brought him here to help her save the house's five new victims. To put an end to the creature, or the house, or the secret society of men who were behind all of it. As difficult as it was to look at his sister's wasting frame, he wondered if he could be as strong as her, or all the others to whom the house had called and who had fought back.

If he were to stay inside Larkspur, could he ever be as brave as Connie? Or would his soul shatter in the way Marcus's had? How much could anybody take before the house changed them forever?

He ran over to the massive double doors at the front of the foyer. Swinging his fists at them, Jason met a powerful force that flung him back down the steps toward Lou.

Fighting felt suddenly pointless.

He stared at his sister. Lou had become a shadow of herself. Shaking, he held back a scream of rage. Jason stretched out on the floor beside her. He didn't care if there was still a barrier between them. He tried to wrap his arms around her, hoping she could still sense that she wasn't alone.

Then, with a shove that felt like a car crash, Jason found himself standing outside the dollhouse again.

"No!" he sobbed, desperate to be by his sister's side. "No, Lou, no . . ." Wiping at his face, he dropped to his knees and peered through the windows into the foyer where Lou was lying at the center of the circular parquet pattern.

It felt like a knife was twisting in his gut. Here was his chance to smash the dollhouse to pieces and break the curse that the society had set in place. But to do so, he'd have to break Lou too.

If he did nothing, he'd have to watch his sister become a pile of bones.

Jason blinked. He'd lost. His sister needed him, and he'd failed her.

A pair of cold hands clutched his shoulders from behind. Sharp fingers wrenched his skin, spinning him around.

CHAPTER 35

"YOU!" JASON'S VOICE was like a howl, reverberating out into the void.

Marcus stared back at him, his expression blank. Jason leapt to his feet and then shoved at his cousin. Marcus stumbled back but stayed on his feet, holding eye contact. "Look what did you did to us!" Jason cried out. "Where is Connie?"

Marcus gestured vaguely off the path. "The house told me I had to get rid of her."

Fire flooded through Jason's veins. He lashed out, beating his fists against Marcus's face and neck and chest. He hit Marcus again and again—so many times that his knuckles ached. Marcus steadied his stance but did not fight back. His body flinched and flailed, but he remained silent, almost calm, as if he knew he deserved each punch. His lack of response only infuriated Jason more.

Jason shouted out between blows, "I want . . . you to feel . . . what Lou feels!"

Marcus stepped aside. Jason missed the mark. His momentum forced him forward, almost off the lighted path. He faced his cousin.

"I can't feel anything anymore," said Marcus. His voice was soft, barely there. "I think that's my biggest problem at the moment."

"Wrong," said Jason. "*I'm* your biggest problem."

Marcus shook his head. "You still don't get it. You haven't seen half of what this place can do. It will take away everything you are. All your hope. All your fear. Scoop out your insides and turn you into a hollow shell."

Jason's vision went blurry. He blinked away tears of rage. "Is that what's happening to Louise right now?" Marcus backed away from the dollhouse, but Jason caught a fistful of his shirt and forced him to peer inside. "Look! That is your cousin! My sister! See what's happening to her. How could you allow this? What's *wrong* with you?"

"I don't know!" Marcus tried to pull away, but Jason held him in place. "I-I'm scared. I've been too scared for too long. I can't take much more."

"Jason!" He heard his father's voice calling out, even though Marcus didn't seem to notice.

Jason understood that soon all this would be gone, along with his sister. The darkness around the dollhouse looked different, more gray than black now. He forced the voice out of his head. "You're not as scared as Lou is right now," he whispered to Marcus. "If you're not going to do anything, then why'd you even show up again?"

The boys stared in through the window. After a few seconds, Marcus hung his head. "What do you expect me to do?"

"I expect you to be brave. With me. Let's go back in there and bring her out."

Marcus released a long sigh. "It won't work," he said. "The creature will never let her go." He paused. "Not unless . . ."

Jason couldn't take his eyes off of Lou. If he didn't already know it was her, he would never have recognized her. She looked like bones and shrunken skin inside her clothes. "Not unless *what*?" he asked. When Marcus didn't answer, Jason turned and found his cousin had vanished. He called out, "Marcus?" Jason peered through the foyer window again and saw him standing alone in the grand foyer.

Jason's heart dropped. How had he gotten inside? Where was Lou?

A groan came from the other side of the dollhouse. He circled around and saw his sister lying on the ground. "Lou!"

Light-headed, he rushed to her, gathering her up in his arms and squeezing her tightly.

The dollhouse shuddered and shook.

"Jason?" Lou asked. "Where are we?"

He held her at a distance and looked her up and down. No longer a rag doll, her cheeks were pink and her frame flush. "Marcus got you out of the house," he said, then hugged her again.

"M-Marcus?" she stammered, pushing him away and trying to stand. "But he's the one . . . The one who . . ."

Jason helped her stand. "I know what he did." He directed her toward the shivering foyer window. Inside, a great black cloud had appeared at the top of the staircase. Marcus stared up at the shadow creature and raised his fists. As the dark mass swooped toward him, he didn't cower. He didn't even scream. He met the thing head-on.

In a blink, it had swirled around him.

CHAPTER 36

"OH, NO!" LOU yelped, covering her mouth.

The dollhouse rattled, the base of it popping up and down against the floor.

The broken walls and fallen roofs rose up, re-forming where they'd crumbled earlier. The creature was using Marcus as its last gasp for survival. Jason closed his eyes, not wanting to imagine what was happening to his cousin.

His father's voice called out from the shadows again, "*Jayyyyyy-sonnnnnn!*"

"Is that Dad?" Lou asked.

A giant spire rose from the center of the house, the tip glistening like a needle.

"We don't have much time," Jason answered. "You know what we have to do?"

Lou nodded. "It's *my* dollhouse. *I* have to break it."

"Can I at least help?"

Lou smiled. "Heck yes."

Together, they leapt at the house. They tore at the turrets and kicked the walls in. Wood splintered, flying in all directions. The miniature furniture scattered into the shadows of the void.

They pounded and stomped and danced on the rubble as gray ash wafted up all around them.

After it was done, Jason and Lou grabbed each other's hands, waiting and watching to see if the debris would move. Rebuild the nightmare. Without the light from within the house, all they could see by now was the pale streak that divided the void in both directions.

Jason noticed that Lou's hand felt strange. Looking down, he saw it was only partially there. His own fingers showed through it. Lou's eyes perked up as she glanced around, seeing a room that Jason could not.

"You're leaving me?" he asked.

She tried to answer, but her voice was already gone. Lou smiled, and he understood.

After his sister disappeared, Jason looked around, expecting to find the walls of the storage room in the condo's basement.

They'd broken the dollhouse after all. But all he saw was the shadow world. The endless dark. The void.

Vague shapes were moving through it.

Some shapes were tall and wide. Others were squat and long. Some made chittering noises. Other sounds were like heavy chains dragging across the ground. There were hard clacks and soft whispers.

The shadow creature's brethren were not pleased with what he and Lou had done to it.

"Dad?" Jason called out, not knowing which way to turn. He hadn't gone through all this only to become some monster's meal. "Dad! Where are you?"

The shapes circled Jason as if he were at the center of their shrinking target.

Jason choked and then tried to call to his dad again, but his voice cracked and crumbled.

A hand clapped the back of his neck.

His father spun Jason around. His eyes were big and worried. "What are you doing down here, buddy? Why weren't you answering me?"

Jason glanced around. "I . . . I . . ." He was standing among the familiar stacks of cardboard boxes, his father staring down at him. The monsters were gone. The cinder block walls had reappeared. A few feet away sat the remains of the dollhouse, jagged pieces of wood sprawled out across the floor. They looked like teeth.

Jason fell into his father's arms, exhausted. He had no vocabulary to explain what he was feeling. His father didn't ask again, but held him close and rubbed at his back, calming his sobs. "Everything will turn out all right, son," he whispered.

Upstairs, a phone was ringing. It took Jason several seconds to recognize the sound. His father squeezed his shoulder and then ran to catch it before it went to voice mail.

Jason followed, closing the storage room door behind him. He checked the knob, making sure it was locked.

He found his father kneeling in the middle of the kitchen floor, his shoulders slumped. One hand covered his face. The other held the phone receiver to his ear. Jason froze, listening to his father's hitching breath, his heart pumping ice water.

Then his father spoke into the receiver, his voice high and wavering. "Louise? Is it really you?"

CHAPTER 37

LOU RETURNED TO California with their mother a couple of days later.

Aunt Paige and Uncle Gilbert continued to communicate with the authorities in Greencliffe. The search for Marcus expanded into the states between Ohio and New York.

Lou and Jason knew how unlikely it was that they'd locate their cousin, but the two kept that to themselves. Shortly after they'd reunited, they decided not to tell their parents what they'd been through.

The fighting had subsided in the time the family had been apart. Lou and Jason were pretty sure that if they added further tales of the cursed dollhouse into the stew, they'd only make their parents worry. After the dollhouse, they knew that worry and fear were what caused the fighting in the first place.

But they had each other—more so now than they ever had before.

One night before school started, Lou woke from a sound sleep.

She found Jason at her door, knocking softly.

"What is it?" she asked blearily. "What's wrong?"

"I need to show you something," he said.

In Jason's room, the light on his bedside table cast a yellow circle across the floor and onto his mattress. Lifting away his pillow, Jason revealed a dried and flattened purple flower.

"Where'd you get that?" Lou asked, wondering why he'd placed it under his pillow. Or what could be so important about it that he'd wake her up in the middle of the night to show it to her. "Did you bring it home from one of your hikes?"

Jason shook his head. "I was half asleep when my hand brushed against it. At first, I thought it was a giant bug. Thankfully not. Do you know what kind of flower it is?"

"I've never seen it before."

He nodded at his phone. "I just looked it up. It's called *larkspur.*"

Lou felt her skin go cold. Like the house? "Throw it away," she said, backing toward his door.

"I don't think I should," he whispered. "I think . . . it's a gift."

"A gift? From who?"

Jason cleared his throat. "From Connie." Lou stared at him like he'd lost his mind. "The original owner of your dollhouse."

"I know who she is, Jay."

He sat on the edge of the bed and stared at her for a few seconds. "There's something I haven't told you."

Lou shivered, her nightgown feeling suddenly thin. "I thought we weren't playing those kinds of games anymore."

"We're not," he insisted. "It's just . . . I didn't want to scare you."

"Scare me . . . *how*?"

Jason sighed. "I've *seen* her. In the mirrors around our house." Lou blinked slowly. "She stands behind me and smiles. She tries to speak but I can't hear what she's saying. Earlier today, I saw her reach into the pocket of her apron and pull out that flower." He pointed at his mattress where the dried, purple plant was lying. "Tonight, I found it here."

"You think she wants to be our friend?"

"Maybe," he said. "But I think it's more than just that."

Lou shook her head, waiting for him to continue.

"When we were together, Connie told me that she could have moved on a long time ago. But she decided to stick around. She promised to stop the house from claiming any more victims. She said that once the evil inside the house was dead, she'd go away, and try to find her mother so they could both be at peace."

"But the house *is* dead," said Lou. "We killed it when we smashed the dollhouse. My heirloom was the last of the marked objects. We broke the curse."

"Did we?" Jason asked. He looked unsure, as if he wished that Lou would give him the answer.

Lou opened Jason's closet door. His laundry bag toppled over and several dirty pairs of socks fell onto the floor.

"What are you doing?" he asked.

She swung the door further, so he could see his reflection in the mirror hanging just inside. "Is she there?"

Jason shook his head. "Not now."

Lou sighed. "Maybe the flower was just her way of saying good-bye."

Jason stared down at it, as if afraid to touch it. "Maybe."

"I wouldn't worry," said Lou. "It's over now. We're safe. Let's go back to bed."

She turned toward his bedroom door. "Lou?" he called out, and she paused. "Would you mind staying here for a little while? Just until I get back to sleep?"

Lou couldn't stop herself from smirking. "My, how things have changed," she whispered.

"Oh, shut it," he said, crossing his arms, frustrated.

Lou crawled across him and stretched out on the other side of his mattress. Jason sighed and lay down beside her.

They stayed that way until dawn, when the sun crept over the crest of Mount Diablo and spilled morning into the valley.

ART CREDITS

ENDPAPERS

Photos ©: 2–3: Larry Rostant for Scholastic; 4 fire: CG Textures; 6–7: Shadow House composite: Shane Rebenschied for Scholastic, Shadow House: Dariush M/Shutterstock, Shadow House fog: Maxim van Asseldonk/Shutterstock, Shadow House clouds: Aon_Skynotlimit/Shutterstock, foreground grass and trees: Maxim van Asseldonk/Shutterstock.

INTERIOR

Photos ©: 24: boy: Keirsten Geise for Scholastic, bird cage: Daft_Lion_Studio/ iStockphoto, ukulele: Keith Publicover/Shutterstock, dollhouse: Larry Rostant for Scholastic, room: Library of Congress; 70–71: pool: Mariusz Niedzwiedzki/ Shutterstock, wheelchair: CatbirdHill/Shutterstock, cart: CG Textures, right shoes: Rainer Fuhrmann/Shutterstock, foreground shoes: Taborsky/ Shutterstock, doll head: AAR Studio/Shutterstock, doll body: Perfect Lazybones/Shutterstock, cloak: Hemera Technologies/Getty Images, cloak stand: JirkaBursik/Shutterstock, broken frame: dimitris_k/Shutterstock, bassinet: iladm/Shutterstock, background doll: unclepepin/Shutterstock, midground doll: Prachaya Roekdeethaweesab/Shutterstock, cat mask: CSA Plastock/Getty Images, books: Paul Orr/Shutterstock; 127: refrigerator interior: Kampol Taepanich/Shutterstock, camera: Kalakutskiy Mikhail/Shutterstock, tunnel: Vladislav S/Shutterstock, refrigerator door: Everett Collection/ Shutterstock, bananas: Maks Narodenko/Shutterstock; 184: book and hands: Namart Pieamsuwan/Shutterstock, frame: Chatchawan/Shutterstock, mantle and candle: Zick Svift/Shutterstock, photograph and clock: CG Textures, sketches: Charice Silverman for Scholastic, girl: robangel69/Fotolia, wallpaper: Larysa Kryvoviaz/Shutterstock; 202–203: dollhouse: Larry Rostant for Scholastic, Shane Rebenschied for Scholastic.

About the Author

Dan Poblocki is the author of many books for young read-
ers, including *The House on Stone's Throw Island*, *The Book of
Bad Things*, *The Nightmarys*, *The Stone Child*, and the Shadow
House series. His novels *The Ghost of Graylock* and *The
Haunting of Gabriel Ashe* were both Junior Library Guild
selections and made the American Library Association's Best
Fiction for Young Adults list. Dan lives in New York's Hudson
Valley, where he spends his time searching for creepy old
mansions like Larkspur House. You can visit him online at
www.danpoblocki.com.

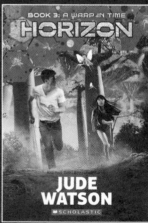

SHADOW HOUSE

DON'T MISS ANY OF THE CHILLING ADVENTURES!

Step into Shadow House.

Enter Shadow House

Each image in the book reveals a haunting in the app.

Search out hidden sigils ◎ in the book for bonus scares in the app.

Step into ghost stories, where the choices you make determine your fate.

CAN YOU ESCAPE?